GECKO TALES

A SHORT STORY COLLECTION

Enjoy
D.S. Fremont

Short and sweet,
Marilyn Hutchison

Jade Johnson

Read on!
Ashleen OGara

Carol Coulter

Enjoy,
D. H. Tremont

TABLE OF CONTENTS

HEARTBREAK MOTEL
by Carol Costa

"This van handles like a dream," Jack told his two companions. "It was sure nice of the company to let us use it."

Frank mumbled his agreement as he leaned forward to turn on the radio. All that emitted from the speakers was loud static.

"Frank, quit messing with that radio," Bob said from the back seat. "We're not going to pick up anything out here in the middle of the desert."

"When Lucy and I went to Palm Springs, we got the oldies station from Phoenix in loud and clear," Frank argued.

Bob laughed. "I suppose that means the poor woman had to listen to Elvis wailing the whole time. You know, if the guy had lived, he'd be in a wheelchair by now, sucking his dinner through a straw."

"And he'd still sound better than those green-haired freaks that scream out lyrics like their pants are on fire," Frank countered, giving up and switching off the radio.

"Okay, guys, knock it off," Jack ordered. "The first weekend we've spent away from our wives in years, and you two have spent the whole time bickering."

"Only because Frankie-boy is stuck in the grooves of those old records he collects.

"I have a very valuable collection," Frank insisted.

To be honest," Jack admitted. "I like Elvis myself. Brings back memories of my youth." He began to sing in a deep baritone voice. "Love me tender, love me true."

Bob leaned forward and yelled in Frank's ear. "Quick, turn the radio back on."

1

Jack stopped crooning and laughed good-naturedly. "You know, Bob, I think you're just sore because your golf scores had more digits than your zipcode."

"I've played better," Bob confessed.

"So has my ten year old son," Frank told him.

Jack and Frank laughed. Bob sat back and pretended to sulk. "Go ahead, enjoy yourselves," he shouted over their chuckles. "Ribbing me is probably a lot more fun than those sand traps you two called home the last two days."

All three of them laughed at that, then Frank peered out the window into the darkness. "Speaking of home, are you sure this is the right road?"

Jack nodded. "Yeah, I'm sure. It used to be the main highway before they built the interstate."

Bob changed the subject back to their weekend's entertainment. "Well, even though my game was a little off, I enjoyed the tournament."

"Me too," Jack agreed. "Is there any coffee left in the thermos?"

Frank picked it up and shook it. "No."

"I don't suppose there's any place to stop on this road, Jack observed. "Hey, wait, what's that sign say up ahead?"

Jack slowed down, so Frank could read the sign on his side of the road. "Good coffee and comfortable beds . . . turn right, three miles. Let's stop and fill up the thermos."

Maneuvering the van onto a side road, Jack followed it for a few miles before they spotted the place advertised on the sign. It was a shabby motel, with a small cafe in front of it. The lights were on in the cafe and there was an open sign in the window, but there were no other cars in the parking lot.

"Looks like a dump," Bob said. "Let's get out of here."

"Oh, quit being so picky," Frank told him. "It's just a little rundown. I need some coffee."

Jack agreed. "Frank's right. Sometimes these out of the way places have the best food."

Bob continued to grumble as Jack parked the van and they piled out. The door to the cafe squeaked loudly when Frank pulled it open. The three of them filed inside and looked around the empty restaurant.

"Just as I thought," Bob complained again. "Standard 1950s right down to the red vinyl and formica tables."

Frank and Jack weren't listening. Their attention had been captured by a group of old photographs hanging on the wall behind an ancient jukebox.

"It's Elvis," Frank cried. "Elvis and some dark-haired lady. Elvis and his guitar. Wow, these are genuine photographs. Hey, who has a quarter? This juke box has some great old tunes."

Before Frank could get a coin for the juke box, a door slammed behind them and an elderly woman dressed in a worn green waitress uniform came out of the back. Her hair was gray, pulled back into a tight bun. She wore wire-rimmed glasses and no make-up. A name tag pinned on her collar identified her as Gertie.

"Well, what do you know," she said. "Real live customers. Welcome to Gertie's Place. How the hell did you find me?"

"We saw your sign on the highway," Jack answered.

She twisted her thin mouth into what could have passed for a smile. "Oh yeah, I forgot about that. My son put it up a few weeks ago. Can't say it's done us much good."

Frank turned from his examination of the juke box. "Where'd you get all these great photographs of Elvis?"

"From him," she replied casually. "Elvis used to be a regular here."

Frank's mouth fell open. "Elvis Presley used to come in here?"

Bob stared at Frank. They had been friends since grade school. He'd always accepted the fact that Frank wasn't too bright, but sometimes even he was amazed at the dumb things that came out of his mouth.

"Get serious, Frank," Bob said. "Elvis Presley wouldn't step foot in a dump like this."

Gertie walked up and confronted Bob. "You callin' me a liar, sonny?"

Jack quickly jumped between them. "No, ma'm. Of course he's not. We've had a long trip, and Bob's just a little grouchy. He doesn't mean anything."

Jack was Bob's brother-in-law, his sister's high school sweetheart. He had started tagging along with Bob and Frank the day after he saved their lives. At least that's how Jack always referred to the incident. Bob maintained that he and Frank could have held their own with the two football players who wanted to use them for punching bags. But they never got the opportunity to find out, because Jack, the team's equipment manager, had stepped in and talked the linebackers into accepting Frank's apology for calling them fumblers after they lost a big game.

Ever since, Jack had been their self-appointed guardian angel. Now as fate would have it, the three men were all employed by one of the largest car dealerships in Southern Arizona. Frank worked in the service department, Jack was a salesman, and Bob headed up the finance department.

Gertie walked over to the window and looked outside. "Is that one of those new vans with a sun-roof and built-in beds?" she asked.

"No ma'am," Jack answered. "That one is last year's model, but a beauty just the same. We work for Harris Chevrolet in Tucson. Our boss let us take one of the loaners to California for a big golf tournament."

"Shut up, Jack. She doesn't care where we're going or where we've been," Bob said.

Gertie looked at Bob. "What's your job at the car lot? Repossessions?"

Bob just grunted and sat down at one of the tables. Jack still in his peacemaker mode, gave her the look that Bob's sister once found irresistible. "How about some coffee and menus?"

"Menus? Where do you think you are, New York City? We ain't got no menus. You eat the specialty of the house or go hungry."

Apparently, other women weren't as impressed with the look.

Across the room, Frank had finally located a quarter and dropped it into the juke box. A scratchy recording of Elvis Presley's *Don't Be Cruel* started to play.

Bob renewed his argument with the old waitress. "What's the specialty of the house, food poisoning?" He laughed at his own joke.

Jack tried to mediate again. "Don't mind him, ma'am. I'm sure the food here is very good. So what is the specialty tonight?"

"I'll have to check with the chef," Gertie told him with a straight face. She turned towards the back where they assumed the kitchen was located.

"Before you go, can we have three coffees?" Jack asked.

"It's there on the back burner, behind the counter. Your leg's not broken. Help yourself, " she called as she continued to depart.

Bob mumbled a curse under his breath and started to get up, but Jack waved him back down. "No problem," he said. "I'll get it."

Jack went behind the counter and rummaged around until he found three cups and filled them with coffee from a glass pot on a hot plate. He brought them over to the table and set them down. Frank was still at the juke box looking at the photos and singing along with Elvis.

'Frank, come on and sit down here and have your coffee," Bob called out. "I want to get out of here."

"I can't stop looking at these photos," Frank called back. "Do you think Gertie would sell me one?"

"That and her first born child. Drink up so we can get out of here. This joint is giving me the creeps. And that old lady is one beer short of a six-pack."

Frank left the photos and sat down at the table. "Just think, Elvis may have sat at this very table," he said.

"Yeah," Jack agreed. "He probably drank coffee from this very cup." He held up the coffee mug he was drinking from.

"Yeah," Frank said. "Trade with me, Jack."

Bob looked at his friends in disbelief. "How do you know he didn't drink out of my cup?" he asked sarcastically. "You are both nuts!"

Gertie returned from her trip to the back room. "How you chumps doing over here?" she asked cheerfully.

"Just peachy," Bob replied in the same sarcastic tone. "But I have a question for you. Is this coffee or boiled tar paper?"

Gertie attempted another smile that didn't quite make it. "Elvis liked it strong and bitter. Used to drink it by the pot full while he strummed his guitar and sang his songs."

Frank almost fell backwards in his chair. "Elvis actually performed here?" he asked, his voice filled with awe.

"That's right, sonny. The sign's all faded now, but this place used to be called Heartbreak Motel."

"Wow!" Frank exclaimed.

"That's really interesting," Jack added.

Bob shook his head and made a face. "For crying out loud, can't you guys tell when someone's pulling your leg? The specialty of this house is Baloney ala Gertie."

"Wrong again," Gertie told him. "Tonight's special is spaghetti and beans. I call it Capone on the Range. Reminds me of the song Elvis used to sing to me after we made love."

Even Frank couldn't swallow that line. "Oh, go on, Gertie. Bob's right. You're just making this all up aren't you?"

"Next time you see Elvis, ask him yourself."

"Elvis is dead," Jack said.

Gertie rolled her eyes. "So that's why he hasn't called me lately."

Bob got to his feet. "Well, thanks for all the laughs, Gertie. Come on, guys, we'd better get going."

"Suit yourself," Gertie said. "That'll be $6.50 for the coffees, tax and tip included."

Bob was the first to react. "$6.50 for three lousy cups of coffee that we had to get for ourselves?" he said angrily.

Gertie shrugged her thin shoulders. "Okay, so forget the tip. That'll be $ 6.00 even."

Jack already had his wallet out. "All I got is a ten . . . you guys got anything smaller?"

6

"Not me," Bob told him.

"I put my last quarter in the juke box," Frank said.

Jack handed Gertie a ten dollar bill.

"Thank you. Have a nice trip," she said, stuffing the ten down the front of her uniform.

"What about my change?" Jack protested.

"Look around, sonny. We ain't had a cash register in here since Elvis wore blue suede shoes."

"He sang a song about those too," Frank commented.

Bob headed for the door. "Let's just get out of here."

"You all come back now," Gertie called after them.

They banged out the door and walked towards the van. Since there wasn't much light in the parking lot, they didn't notice the flat tires until they were on top of it.

"Oh no! Look at the back tires. They're both flat," Jack shouted.

Since the van only had one spare, this was a real problem.

Bob stormed back into the cafe and found Gertie sitting at the counter with her arms folded. "Where's your telephone?"

"It's out of order," she said pleasantly. "Anyway, I would think a hot shot like you would have one of those cellular phones."

She was right, all three of the men had cellular phones. Rather than bring all three, Frank had been elected to carry his. Only he accidentally left it on all afternoon, and ran down the battery. They were stranded.

As if reading his mind, Gertie said. "I made up one of the rooms with nice clean sheets just this afternoon. You want to rent it or sleep in your van out there?"

Bob went back outside to talk to Frank and Jack. It was almost midnight and chances of them being able to walk back to the main highway and catch a ride were slim.

"Doesn't Gertie have a car?" Frank asked.

"She said her son took it. He'll be back in the morning and give us a ride into the next town to get a tow truck or some new tires," Bob told them.

"How much is she going to charge us?" Jack asked, remembering the ten dollars he paid for three cups of coffee.

"She's only got one room made up, and it's thirty dollars for the night."

That sounded reasonable, so they got their luggage from the van. Gertie gave them a key and directions to their room.

"This place sure is old. Do you think Elvis really stayed here?" Frank said after they got inside the room.

"His name was on the guest register," Jack teased.

"I'm going to take a shower," Bob said. "Throw that extra blanket and pillow on the floor for me. You two can have the beds. Elvis probably slept in both of them."

Bob took his last pair of clean underwear out of his bag and went into the bathroom. Jack settled down on one of the beds, while Frank walked around the room, opening the drawers on the battered dresser and looking inside.

"What are looking for, Frank?" Jack finally asked.

Frank had moved to the nightstand. "Nothing, just looking is all. Hey, here's a Bible . . . and there's a letter inside." Frank quickly read the letter. "Hey, Jack, listen to this . . . . To Whom It May Concern, if you are staying in this motel you are in danger. This is the Bates Motel, the one they made the movie about. Stay out of the shower."

Jack laughed out loud. "Oh, Frank, don't be so gullible. The Bates motel didn't really exist, and Psycho was a fictional story, wasn't it?"

It was then that the pipes banged, and Bob began to yell loudly. "No! Ouch! Ouch! Aah!"

"Someone is trying to kill Bob," Frank shouted. He jumped up and ran towards the bathroom with Jack right behind him.

One good push and the old door caved in. The noise scared Bob so badly, he thought he was going to have a heart attack. When he realized that it was Frank and Jack he cursed and screamed at them to get out.

A few minutes later, with a thin towel draped around his waist, Bob was still screaming and cursing.

"Sorry, Bob," Frank said. "The way you were yelling we thought you were in trouble."

"You scared the hell out of us," Jack agreed. "Why were you yelling?"

"Because in the middle of my shower the water turned ice cold," Bob said.

"Oh . . . well," Frank stammered. "Sorry for barging in on you, but we really thought you were in trouble."

"I'm in trouble, all right," Bob yelled again. "Stuck in the middle of nowhere with a demented old woman, and you two."

"Show him the letter, Frank," Jack said indignantly.

Frank handed Bob the letter he found in the bible. Bob quickly scanned it. "It's a joke," he said, crushing the paper into a wad. "I can't believe you guys are taken in by this stuff. First Elvis Presley, now Psycho."

"We're just nervous because of the flat tires," Jack said. "And too much sun this weekend. It's got us all tired out."

"Right. Let's just get some sleep," Bob suggested. All the anger had gone out of him, and he was sorry he had yelled at his friends. He was really lucky to have good friends like Frank and Jack.

"I can't sleep right now," Frank said. "I've got to calm down. I'm going outside for a breath of air."

"Good idea," Jack agreed. "I'll go with you."

Frank yanked the door open, and then screamed like a woman. Jack looked over his shoulder and slammed the door shut.

Bob's heart couldn't take much more of this. "Now what's wrong?" he yelled.

"He's out there, dangling from the roof," Jack whispered.

"Who's out there?" Bob demanded.

"Elvis Presley!" Frank answered.

"No," Jack shouted. "It's the psycho."

"I thought they called him the King," Bob said sarcastically.

Jack shook his head. He was very upset. "Not Elvis, the guy who stuck the knife in him."

9

Bob pushed past them and flung the door open. Elvis Presley, dressed in gold lame, was hanging over the porch with a knife sticking out of his chest. Bob walked over for a closer look.

"It's only a dummy dressed up like Elvis," he shouted back at his friends.

Moving cautiously, Frank and Jack came outside and saw that Bob was right.

"It is a dummy," Jack agreed. "Stuck with a knife and splattered with ketchup."

"Another one of Gertie's jokes," Bob said. "I swear you two will fall for anything."

"Well, I've had enough of this old lady and her sick jokes," Frank cried. "I say we get out of here."

"If we go real slow, we can drive on the flat tires," Jack reasoned. "It'll ruin them, but I'd rather buy new tires than spend another minute in this place."

"It's not that far to the main highway. We can get help there," Bob agreed.

They went back inside to get their luggage. As they were gathering it, they heard the roar of an engine and a horn honking. Bob rushed back to the porch just in time to see the tail lights of their van disappear into the night.

The next morning, Bob, Jack, and Frank, walked backed to the main highway and caught a ride into the next town, where they reported the theft of the van to the local police, and rented a car to drive home in.

Bob dropped Jack off at his house. "Now don't worry, Bob. I'm sure the police will find the van," his brother-in-law told him for the fiftieth time that day.

"It doesn't matter," Bob said in a steel-edged voice. "The van was fully insured. What does matter is that no one ever find out how the three of us were conned by an old lady. I'd be the laughing stock of the office."

"I didn't think loan officers were allowed to laugh," Frank said.

"They're not," Bob replied icily. "What's our cover story?"

"We stopped for coffee, and while we were inside drinking it, someone hot-wired the van and stole it from the parking lot," Jack repeated.

"Right. See you tomorrow."

Of course the police and the insurance company had the real story and a full description of Gertie and Bob was sure they would keep it all confidential. Back at work, Bob, Jack, and Frank took a lot of ribbing about losing the company van, but they all stuck to the same story and after a few weeks, the incident began to fade away.

It might have been forgotten entirely if not for one little thing. Two months later, Gertie strolled into Harris Chevrolet and asked to test-drive a new van, one with a sun-roof and built-in beds.

Bob and Jack both had the day off, so Gertie might have gotten away with it except for one thing. Frank was on his way back to the service department after lunch, when he saw Gertie on the lot. She looked a lot different with her hair dyed black, no glasses, skillfully applied make-up and fashionable clothes, but Frank recognized her immediately and called the police.

Later that evening, Jack and Bob went to Frank's house to get the full story.

"She looks completely different," Jack exclaimed as Gertie's photo was shown on the six o'clock news. "How did you know it was her?"

"Yeah," Bob agreed. "I wouldn't have recognized her. How did you?"

Frank grinned. "I've been looking at photographs of her with dark hair, no glasses, and nice clothes for two months."

"What photographs?" Bob asked.

Frank smiled and motioned for his two friends to follow him. He led them through the kitchen into the workshop he had set up in his garage. There hanging on the wall over his tool bench were two nicely framed photographs.

Jack leaned over the bench for a better look. "Hey, those are the ones that were hanging over the jukebox in that broken down diner," he said.

"That's right," Frank replied, smugly. "Gertie and Elvis Presley. Guess she didn't lie about everything."

SECRET INGREDIENT

by Mary Ann Hutchison

So this is how it ends? Sheesh. Of all the ways I thought I'd go, this one wasn't even in the running! I envisioned a small group of loved ones surrounding my bed, quietly weeping as I murmured last words of wisdom before departing. Instead, my last words were: "why, you son-of-a bi – ."

It's taken me a few minutes to get used to death mode, but I kinda like it. Surprise, Daniel. I can see you, and I can talk to you, but you can't see or hear me. Well, that's not quite true. You are standing over my body, with that stupid "deer-in-the-headlights" look on your face. The one you always chose when you couldn't get your way. The one you always wore after we fought about THE recipe. MY recipe.

Yeah, that's right, get a towel and wipe the blood off of your hands. Don't bother trying to wipe your fingerprints off the weapon. They all saw you. All fifty thousand plus of our devoted fans. The ones who tuned in to see me. Not you. And for those who didn't catch today's "Cooking With Doris and Daniel At Noon" segment, there'll be the instant replay on tonight's news.

You always thought you were better than me. Or is that I? Sure, you've got those cooking school diplomas hanging on the wall from the Culinary Institute and the Cordon Bleu in Paris. Big deal. The ribbons lining my office walls were earned for my creativity. Not yours! You hated that, didn't you, Daniel? Just couldn't stand it.

No matter how hard you tried, you never could guess the secret ingredient in THE recipe. It was simple, really. Had you just given it a bit more thought. Had you given me just a little more time. We were gonna hit it big. The contract is all ready for us to sign. Right now, it's sitting on top of your desk, wrapped as an anniversary present. The fifth anniversary of our partnership, Daniel. I was going to take you with me, all the way to the top. You and me, kid. Our very own nationally syndicated TV show on the Food Channel. Better than Bobby Flay and Rachel Ray put together. Doris and Daniel's Delectables on national television; no more small time stuff for us. Product placement, cookbooks. We could've had it all, baby.

Instead, you're going to be preparing gallons of watery soup in the state prison kitchen, until they roast your butt with gas. That's the preferred method of execution in Arizona. How ironic – you always did prefer cooking with gas. By the way, congratulations on your choice of weapons – a four-inch meat probe straight to the heart. A butcher knife would've been too ordinary.

I suppose I shouldn't have called you an idiot while we were on the air. But Daniel, even an amateur cook could've guessed that the secret ingredient is black cardamom. Black cardamom, stupid; not green. And you call yourself a chef!

PERFECT
by Jude Johnson

"I can't believe I'm here, Therese," Maggie Pearce told the happy woman beaming beside her on the New York sidewalk across from the Ziegfeld Theater. "I've never been a 'fan-girl' of anyone's before, let alone some obscure Brit actor. Imagine flying clear across the country for this! I must be nuts. Are we even sure he's going to show?"

"Yep." Therese Esposito nodded, fluffing her dark curls. "Lisa Kaye works for a PR firm and talked to the management people herself. Helps to have connections, doesn't it?" She smiled. "C'mon Maggie, it'll be worth it! Aren't you glad we all connected on the Internet? People from all over the freakin' world can chat about a shared interest. And now we've met each other in person at last. Besides, how often do you get a chance to go to a World Premiere?" She elbowed Maggie gently. "Just think—John Harrison, People Magazine's 'Sexiest Brit in Breeches' right here, in real life!" She smiled, grey eyes twinkling. "Bet he comes over to sign autographs!"

"No way." Maggie shook her head. "We may be in the front row behind these barricades but we're clear across the street from the theater."

"Ah, but we have signs." Karen stood next to Therese, holding a poster stapled to a yardstick. "He'll know we're his loyal Internet fans. Who else is here for him but us?" She looked up and down the street. "In fact, there really aren't that many people here for a premiere. Kinda lets you know this film's not that big of a deal, certainly not a major summer blockbuster." Thick blond hair trailed down the back of Karen's chic, sleeveless black dress. She smiled broadly. "Plus we all look awesome. He'll love this, wait and see."

Maggie had to admit they did make a smart-looking group. Ten members of their Internet group had gathered from across the country.

Now they waited, neatly attired, excitement brightening their faces, a few placards bearing John Harrison's name adorning the steel barricade.

She brushed the skirt of her stretchy black velvet dress, pleased with how it hugged her in just the right places in a classic silhouette. The neckline showed a mere hint of cleavage, and the way the skirt moved when she walked secretly made her want to spin around like a little girl in a fancy new Easter dress. She felt prettier than she had in ages—especially when a few of the handsome men walking past in business suits smiled at her.

Suddenly a long sleek limo pulled up and stopped at the end of the red carpet. Photographers' flashes lit the early evening twilight and everyone in the crowd around them craned their necks to get a glimpse.

"Never mind, it's just one of those Olsen twins." Karen waved one manicured hand in dismissal.

"Which? Omigod, she looks like her head's two sizes too big for her neck." Therese frowned. "Somebody feed that girl some linguine and sausage, quick."

The Girls—their Internet group moniker—laughed.

"She'd never even sniff a plate of pasta. She might gain an ounce," Karen observed. "Anyway, we have time before we really need to pay attention. I've been to a ton of these premieres. As one of the leads, John won't arrive right off. The bigger roles show up closer to screening time, so Pete Ralston and Kate Lewis will likely be the last to get here."

"Think John'll be with You-know-who?" Andrea, another New Yorker further down the row, leaned forward to ask.

"Go ahead and use her real name," Therese teased. "Bitch Voldemort."

"An evil wizard bent on destroying the world could still act better than Brigitte DuBois," Karen chuckled. "Since that Frenchie latched her hooks into John while they were making this film, she's never let him go anywhere alone. And she always poses bent forward with her boobs hanging low and her mouth wide open like a porn star. Gross."

"Did everyone read that interview she gave yesterday? She swears she's this generation's Brigitte Bardot." Andrea laughed. "As if anyone knows who that is."

"Dear God, you younger people have no sense of cinematic history." Stephanie, a plump brunette from Detroit, shook her head. "Bardot was the sex kitten of the fifties and sixties. DuBois is nowhere near as attractive, in my opinion. As an actress she's too wooden to play a fence post. I still don't see what John finds so enthralling about her. She's rude and cuts him down in those online interviews."

Maggie shrugged. "Opposites attract and all—hey, is that Katie Couric—or Ellen DeGeneres?"

They peered at the crowd filling the end of the red carpet until they satisfied their curiosity.

One of the other Girls spoke. "I wish John had hooked up with Kate Lewis instead of that DuBois—she's a good actress and she's not into the celeb lifestyle," Polly said in her South Philly accent. "They'd make a cute couple, doncha think?"

"Yes, but she was married when they started filming," Stephanie replied. "Poor thing; her husband died in that plane crash on his way to visit her on the set in Vancouver. Now she lives in San Diego; just got engaged to that multimillionaire baseball player. Too bad he's on the road with the team somewhere. He's very handsome; I wouldn't mind seeing him."

"Baseball players are like camels—they spit." Therese said. "I'm hoping John Harrison shows up in a tight pair of breeches."

"This film 'French Pastry' could very well tank with DuBois as the leading lady," Karen said.

"She's supposed to be some big star in France, but every movie of hers I've seen stinks. Her characters are always topless and moaning, looking totally bored," Polly added.

Karen nodded and continued. "While Kate Lewis is especially big now with her TV show, and Ralston's been the hot Irish stud this winter, this is John's first lead role since the Aussie historical series. I'm kinda worried for him; it's not a good sign when a movie's sat on the shelf for four years."

"Are we gonna actually see it?" Andrea looked puzzled. "We don't have tickets, do we?"

"No," Jayne replied. "We're just here to cheer John on and show the suits in charge he has an active fan base." She gestured to the north. "Once they're all inside the theater, we can go up 54th to The Castle. See the pub sign right there? If we get a table on the second floor, we'll have a view of the front of the theater when the movie's over and see him leave for the after-party." She winked and grinned like the devil's own daughter. "We might talk the security guys into letting us in if we show up. They're usually off-duty NYPD. I have a few friends who work those shifts; they've let me in before. Never hurts to ask."

"This right here is perfect for me. I'll see the movie when I get home. Hell, I'd pay to see John read the phone book." Maggie grinned and shifted her weight. Her feet ached from standing on the concrete all afternoon. But she could handle a little discomfort for a glimpse of her favorite actor in person. Like Therese said—when would she get another chance?

Karen shouted the alert. "Oh my God! Here they are! There's What's-her-face, and—"

"—John! John, over here!" Maggie found herself yelling along with Therese and everyone else, waving wildly and grinning.

John Harrison followed his blonde girlfriend out of the limo. Ignoring the PR handlers waiting at the end of the red carpet, he strode across 54th Street, leaving Brigitte DuBois standing alone, her wide red mouth agog.

Maggie stared. Holy Cow! Could a real man truly be that beautiful? Hair the color of toasted coconut cascaded to the top edge of his tux collar in a thick mass of natural curls. There was a tinge of coppery color to his smooth skin—not quite tan, but not vampire pale. A healthy glow, Maggie decided. He wore no tie with the exquisite raw silk shirt of pearl white; it lay enticingly open at the throat. The luxurious black jacket gleamed in the waning twilight across broad shoulders.

18

She vaguely recalled reading something about how he'd played rugby at school, and noticed the athletic way he trotted across the street like a powerful horse barely reined in check. And those pants fit like a tailor's lifetime achievement—not too baggy and not obscenely tight—a celebration of muscular male physique. She watched him start at the furthest end of the barricade from her, signing anything and everything presented to him.

His British baritone was unmistakable and familiar. "Saw those signs and had to come over, didn't I? Thank you so much. You stood out here how long? Oh bless, then. Right bunch of supporters I've got, haven't I? Thank you all, truly."

"Any news on a sequel to 'The Sydney Settlers' yet?" Therese called out.

"No, I'm afraid not. The Arts Network seems to have changed their focus to reality Dog Hunting. They withdrew their half of the funding. But there's always hope someone else might pick it up, isn't there?" John smiled in her direction. Rich chocolate eyes twinkled, framed in dark brown lashes.

"What about that movie for The Hallmark Channel—'Autumn Rain?'" A young man standing behind them called out. "Have you signed on to play Keith yet?"

"How on earth do you people find out about these things? It's early days, but I'm hoping to see the script next month." The small crowd applauded and hooted their approval. John made his way along until he caught Maggie's eye. He stopped and held her gaze for a long second before returning his attention to Polly and signing the book she held out to him.

"How 'bout a kiss, John?" Polly asked, blushing.

"And why not?" Laughing, he obliged, quickly bussing her proffered cheek, then Andrea's.

"Omigod, omigod, omigod . . . ." Therese started hyperventilating as he neared.

Then suddenly he stood in front of Maggie, staring into her eyes. Something passed between them. Something rare and weird and magical.

He gazed at her as if no one else existed before leaning in. Marble smooth skin grazed her cheek and Maggie closed her eyes when warm lips pressed lightly. She caught a hint of cologne at once memorable and right; exactly as he should smell.

He inhaled and nuzzled her slightly. She lifted her chin and touched her nose to his cheek in response, as though taking part in a ritual they'd shared many times before.

That's ridiculous, her rational mind interjected. You've never met the man.

Shut the hell up and let me enjoy this, the dreamer in her heart replied.

Then he withdrew. Her lids lifted slowly to see him smiling at her, bemused.

"Something to sign, love?" he asked in a soft voice.

"Oh! Uh, yeah, uh-huh." She handed him her book.

"Everyone have this same one—'The Making of Sydney Settlers'— do you?" He flipped through the pages, his head cocked to the right. "Oh dear, I remember the day we shot this scene. This is a terrible picture, me all wet and dripping like a near-drowned cat. Colder than Scotland in January, it was. I had to dive into that pond over and over because the locals wouldn't cooperate and stay out of the shot. Had a horrific chest cold for weeks after—all for what eventually amounted to a thirty-second scene."

"Was it worth it?" she asked.

His dark eyes gleamed. "Did you enjoy it?"

"I did. Very much."

"Then"—he wriggled his brows and winked, then carefully signed the page—"it was absolutely most definitely worth it." He handed the book back, taking her hand.

Electricity shot through, speeding her heart in a way no static shock ever had.

He lifted her hand to his lips, bestowing a light kiss and never taking his eyes from hers. Still holding her hand, he leaned forward and spoke in an intimate, low voice. "Lovely, so lovely to see you—again, is it? Forgive me, I seem to have forgotten your name."

"Maggie," she choked out as warm lips touched her cheek once more.

"Thank you, Maggie. I look forward to when we meet again. And I do hope it's soon." He pulled away and flashed his eyes at her before stepping back and addressing the group. "Thank you all so very much for being here. You've made this evening ever so perfect."

With a smile, John Harrison waved to his well-wishers and ran back across the street. But he turned and blew a kiss toward The Girls before Brigitte DuBois decidedly took his arm and yanked him onto the red carpet amid a flurry of photographer's flashes.

Maggie realized she hadn't been breathing. She gulped a big lungful of New York exhaust fumes and launched into a bladder-threatening coughing fit.

Therese threw her arm around her and hugged tight. "You see?" she grinned, teary. "Told you he'd come over!"

"Awesome!" Karen grinned, laughing. "Was this not the best fan experience ever?"

"Perfect," Maggie nodded, touching her cheek. "Ever so."

"Perfect" is an excerpt from Desire—A Dangerous Dance, *Book One in a ballroom dancing series by Jude Johnson currently in the works.*

WALK
by Ashleen O'Gaea

On this, his four thousand, nine hundredth walk, Sammy is no less eager to set out than on his first.

It has been several days since he's been out. He hasn't felt good for the last week or so, but when he doesn't, they take one of those great rides to the vet's — all rides in cars are great, and all the vet techs are his friends — and they pet him and pet him. After a long nap at the vet's, he feels much better.

On the way home, when the car ride is even better, Amanda still isn't too cheerful. Sammy thinks she needs petting, too, and he keeps his paw on her lap all the way home. He sees her talking to him, moving her mouth to shape words. She's unable to speak right now, but Sammy doesn't know that; his hearing is pretty well gone. He doesn't notice because he can remember, for instance, the words that go with Amanda's gestures.

Hopping up and down and batting at her foot means, "Hold on, boy, hold on! Got a rock in my shoe; wait a minute . . . oof!" Bending down and reaching toward his muzzle with grabbing fingers means "No eat!"

On this, Sammy's four thousand, nine hundredth walk, the lingering blossoms on the low-hanging mesquite branches are strongly fragrant, but they don't overpower the various messages that were left some days ago. As the older scents fade, nuances can be gleaned. The new ones' complexity isn't immediately evident, but their headlines are always of interest.

Today, they recall dim memories of other streets, and different signatures in different sands. He stands for a long time, remembering —

and maybe resting a little, too – and then he's ready to walk a little farther.

A dead snake! Amanda, as usual, tries to distract him. He isn't much interested; how many had he seen in his day? He looks at this one, but he doesn't argue with Amanda about giving it a wide berth. Anyway, she's not as easy to tug around on the leash anymore, so today he thinks he'll just let her go where she wants to.

But before Amanda wants to go in another direction, Sammy manages a bite of something, something hidden in the fallen palo verde flowers that he likes to search beneath. He chooses not to translate the grabbing fingers and ignores her "No eat!" command, just this once.

There is also something left of a dead bird in the middle of the street, but it's old and flat and too spoiled by tires to be worth an extra fifteen or twenty steps.

Sammy doesn't hear the fanfares of dove-coos that herald his passage down the street, but he feels a slight wave of air, and the startlement of a dozen or more doves catches his eye. One more after the others have flown triggers another memory: these are things he used to chase across the yard, them and their shadows. He is pleasantly surprised to remember the taffeta crush of the birds' wings and Amanda's delighted laughter.

Amanda thinks, when he gazes into empty air, that he's scenting the neighborhood, discerning yards with dogs from those without, and she isn't wrong about that. But she doesn't understand that he is reveling, too, in the various textures beneath his calloused paws.

Very soft sand; sand with bits of mica and little rocks in it. Thick yellow blossoms, damp and crunchy at the same time. Dirt verges layered with years of pine needles.

Asphalt, which feels different in the shade than in the sun. The cement skirts of driveways that punctuate the street; dazzling white-rock deltas that emerge, instead of cement, from some yards.

Pebbles that in some places along their various routes come right to the edge of the street, and in other places yield to bigger rocks that

23

challenge his balance but offer no threat to the soft spots between his toes.

A few paces around one corner they turn every now and then, there's grass, green grass, moist and soft. Amanda does understand, at least, what a joy it is to walk on that.

She understands, too, that he needs to take a lot of time at one particular tangle of dry grass and weeds that grows under the mesquite at the mouth of the wash. Every dog and coyote, every skunk and coati and javelina, stops there and leaves word for everyone else.

"I am in my prime!"

"Just finished mating!"

"Looking for a good time? I'm in heat!"

"I'm old, but not out of the game."

After making sure of his balance on the hummock, he leaves his own few drops of announcement, too. "I'm fourteen. What game is that, again?"

Today when they stop at the intersection of the wash and the road, he gazes westward. His vision is still fine, but a slight rise and a gentle curve keeps him from seeing the end of the street. He knows what's over there, though. A wall of oleander, sheltering a disused community swimming pool; beyond that, abandoned tennis courts, and then a great open space.

He has always wondered, and in his dreams imagines, what it would be like to run off-leash there. Amanda has once or twice seen this question in his eyes, and told him that it would certainly be wonderful – except for the cholla buds dotting the ground, and the busy street into which he would undoubtedly bound, oblivious.

On the way home, they walk by the Bunny Lawn. The bunnies scatter long before he gets within leash-length of them, but he can smell the oil in their fur, and the blood in their long, thin-skinned ears, and he can see their white little cotton-tails hopping into the bushes that border the grass.

"Not our yard," Amanda tells him, for almost the five-thousandth time. He has never dug into the bunnies' burrows to meet them, but today he comes as close to them as he ever has. He can smell Amanda's amazement that they waited so long to bolt, and that one of them only half-conceals itself and watches as she leads Sammy by.

It is warm, but not panting-hot. There is just enough moisture in the air to hold a delicate gumbo of delightful scents, from their route and from the branching streets they do not venture down this afternoon. No other dogs are out to challenge his conviction that this neighborhood is his and his alone. He is unaware, as he often is, that Amanda sees a man out walking his dog, too; she turns upwind before Sammy notices.

As they sidle into his yard again, cutting across the front toward the gate in the fence, he sees that ground squirrels and doves scatter, as they should, before his dominance. Lizards shoot away from him too, and he nods that it is well that they do. He's sure he's still quick enough to drop a hunter's paw on their tails. He pauses for a moment, pretending to be a pointer and eyeing a cactus wren that ignores him until the last possible moment.

Out of habit, Sammy stops for a moment when Amanda opens the gate, so she can close it again behind them. With some satisfaction, he remembers what he knows she's saying now: "That's right, wait just a minute. Goooood dog. Good boy!" He knows she is saying it because she is patting his head as she speaks, and there is a little extra vibration – all that passes for sound now – in her hand. Good Amanda, he thinks.

The water bowl by the house is freshly filled; it's something Phil does while Amanda walks the dog. Sammy laps eagerly. Fresh water. What a luxury. He knows it to be rare; he never encounters any water at all on his walks. There are times, as when they pass the Bunny Lawn, that he can smell water nearby in time and space. But only here at home is it in a bowl for him to drink, as much as he ever wants, and more if he empties the bowl.

He looks to his own small patch of lawn, and thinks he might just have a little roll. He can't fling himself down as he used to do; his back hurts if he does that, so he lowers himself carefully. Once he's on the grass, he has to roll slowly, but that's no hardship. It feels good, and slow makes it even better.

In the old days, Sammy remembers, he played in the sprinkler. Water is hard to catch but great fun to chase. He lolls onto his side, content today to nuzzle the grass and enjoy the smell of its summer growth spurt. No need to thrust his sore hip hard enough to turn over completely.

Through closing eyes he sees Amanda going back into the house, smiling at him over her shoulder. He heaves himself to his feet, waits for the discomfort in his joints to settle, and follows her. She holds the door for him. Then, because he can see his cookie box from where he's standing, he trots over to it, checking if it's time for one.

He gives Amanda his best cookie-look, and her expression of – worry? – softens. Yes! Cookie time! Gooooood Amanda! When his tail stops wagging and his hind legs find their balance again, he takes it gently from her hand. As he adjusts it between his teeth, he notices that it doesn't smell or taste quite as good as he expects it to. Ah, well. Maybe if he lays it on the carpet for a few minutes, it will be more appealing.

He takes the cookie to the living room and sets it down. He looks at it, and doesn't really feel like a cookie right now. Maybe just a little lie-down first, and he looks at his bed, but it's not where he wants to be.

Amanda is sitting on the couch. He goes over to her and lays his head in her lap. He sees her lips moving and knows she's telling him he's a good boy, and that of course she'll help him up onto the couch. And she does.

He takes a few steps, finding his cushion legs, and settles himself with his hip resting on hers. She's a little bony, but this position is good for his back, at least for a few minutes.

His right front paw twitches as he remembers a few steps of their walk. It was a good one: down to the corner, around to the pee bushes, and home again. There'd been a dead snake, and bunnies, and some little illicit morsel.

Maybe on their next walk – that would be his four thousand, nine hundred and first – they'll go up that hill past the wash, around the tennis courts, and to that open space. Maybe traffic will be light and Amanda will let him off the lead. Just once. He'll watch out for the cholla buds and the cars, he really will. His back legs twitch in anticipation. Just once.

He isn't looking at Amanda's face now, and even though she's petting him, through his thick fur he can't feel her talking.

"Oh . . . ." She buries her face in Sammy's neck and unbuckles his collar. Some of his fur starts to glisten with her tears.

"Amanda?"

She looks at Phil. "I'm glad I took him out today. I wasn't sure he could make it, but he really wanted to go, and . . . ." She pauses and takes a deep breath. "He . . . he had a really good time. We couldn't go very far, but — well, now he can go as far as he wants to." She gives up trying to talk.

"Amanda?"

"He's gone, Phil," she whispers. "Our old Sammy-dog, he's gone."

He's off lead at last, with no traffic in sight, and he hears the doves hail his fleetness across the open space, too light-footed for the cholla buds.

INSANITY BY DEGREE
by D. H. Tremont

"Insanity is measured by degree. The yardstick by which your own should be measured is by the amount of trouble you get into in any given moment, my dear Dani," Enrico said as he grabbed the paper out of my hand. He was on his mobile phone and calling for police back-up as he grabbed his navy blazer and bolted out the door. I was right behind him.

I stepped in front of the car and banged on the hood to get him to stop. "Oh no you don't, Inspector Moravia. Where you go I go!"

"Dani, Mario told you that Tito is acting like a madman. There is no way I want you there. This is police business. You could get hurt."

"Oh, shut up. I am going – so just drive," I said as I slammed the car door shut.

"From what I could get from your end of the conversation, Tito Scarlatti is on a rampage because his granddaughter was missing – right?"

"Yes."

"Yes. Yes is the only word you have to say?" He raked his fingers through his dark brown hair. "Damn you, woman. You invited me for a relaxing lunch and have now embroiled me in God knows what," Enrico said as he threw the car in reverse. "Would you mind giving me more information – dearest?"

"I hate your sarcasm, Enrico."

"Daphne Daniela Palmer, you are trying my patience."

"Oh. You the most patient of men."

"Bloody hell!" Enrico yelled

"You promised not to yell," I yelled back.

He bit his lip and looked at me for a second and turned to face forward. "Yes, I did, but I will again if you continue your sarcasm – understood? No, don't answer." He mumbled under his breath and I could tell he was saying words I would not want to hear so I kept quiet. "Now, we'll try again," Enrico said as he drove up the narrow drive to the main road. "What did Mario tell you – you know the parts of the conversation I did not hear?"

"Mario told me that he was worried because Tito had discovered where Angelina had been taken and was heading that way."

"The address on this paper," he said as he waved the 'post it' at me. "Go on . . . tell me more." Enrico raced through the snarled Roman traffic.

"Tito got in the gun case and when Mario and Lucia tried to stop him he fired at them," I said as I closed the clasp on the seat belt. "Oh, and did I tell you that Mario said that when Tito stormed out of the house he took all of the car keys?"

"Wonderful. That means they won't be getting there anytime soon." As he concentrated on driving he pounded out a number on his mobile phone and barked orders to someone at headquarters.

As he relayed the information I was musing over what he had said to me about the measurement of insanity in my life. His reference to my propensity to get into trouble was somewhat accurate – no, totally justified because I knew this was going to be an ugly scene.

"Enrico, I remember this place," I said as we drove down the tree-lined graveled path. "This is the country villa that the Scarlattis use for guests and out-of-town clients. Look over there – that's Tito's Mercedes."

Enrico was out of the car and dashing in the front door before I could get out of the seatbelt. Once inside the large villa it took me only a few moments to figure out that Enrico had headed down the stairs to the workshop area. I bumped into him as I rushed down the circular stairs. He motioned to me to be quiet. We stood still and looked at the scene before us.

The lighting came from skylights positioned at either end of a huge rectangular studio. Bookcases lined two walls at the end of the space where workbenches, stools and instruments were located. Photographic equipment was strewn everywhere. The other portion of the large room had been turned into an informal seating space. Two large overstuffed chairs and a sofa with brown faded corduroy were positioned in the center with a 60" round table that served not only as a place to eat but a horizontal expanse to deposit magazines and clutter.

Tito stood poised with his finger on the hammer of a 35 Magnum. The glint of hatred from his hooded dark eyes asked for release – no, demanded it. His granddaughter, Angelina, lay on a sky blue velvet chaise lounge near the far wall between the two portions of the room. She was naked and unconscious. Her pale blond hair draped across the cushions and cascaded to the floor. Her breathing was labored.

There was a pungent, almost mold like stench mixed with that of marijuana and other chemical smells. There was loud music playing with a bass beat that was repetitive and agitating.

Two naked men were sitting on cushions leaning against the wall near the chaise in a drug stupor, but obviously conscious enough to realize that Tito and his gun were a real threat. Between the men and Angelina drug apparatus was strewn on side tables and the floor.

Fabio was cowering in the corner. "Papa, ti prego . . . ."

"Silenzio, stronzo. Speak English. I want your bastard friends to understand why they will die."

"No. You don't understand – she came to us and wanted the drugs." Fabio tried to explain.

With a wave of the gun Tito shouted, "Silenzio"

Tito found the CD player and ripped out the CD that was playing. There was silence. Once the music stopped I felt relieved to have the incessant drone gone. I had sensed that this noise had only agitated Tito more. I hoped that the quiet would help him to regain his composure.

My hope was destroyed when Tito screamed at Fabio, "Answer me the one question I asked you – did you rape her also?"

"No, God — no!"

"You allowed these pigs to touch her?"

It was with this question that I understood the extent of Tito's fury; I understood that Fabio had in his drug frenzied stupor allowed two of his friends to rape Angelina. What folly had possessed me to think that by my coming with Enrico to this nightmarish scene, I would be able to fix the unfixable? I knew that I understood Tito's fury because I had a seething knot in my solar plexus; if I felt such anguish in my own breast, I could not fathom what galloped through Tito's brain and coursed through his body stirring a tidal wave of retribution.

As I stood assessing the situation, I knew that, within a short time, something awful was going to happen. I also knew that if it was Enrico's goal to stop a murder it was to my mind an almost impossible task.

Enrico slowly walked down the stairs as he said, "Tito, put the gun down. We need to calmly discuss this." He was able to get to the bottom of the staircase before Tito's glare of hatred and gun were leveled at Enrico. "You were not to come here, Ispettore Moravia. You must leave. This is of the family."

"You need to put the gun down, Tito."

"Ispettore, this pig and the slime on the floor do not deserve to live." Tito turned and focused his aim toward Fabio. Fabio urinated as he turned white and started to whimper and groveled on his knees. Tears streamed down his face.

With disgust Tito said, "Stand up and die like a man – you bastard."

I dashed down the stairs and rushed to Tito's side as he put the gun to Fabio's head. "Tito, he is your son – stop – you must stop."

Without moving the gun or diverting his stare, he said, "In ancient Roman times the father was allowed to kill any child who did not function in society with honor. He must die."

I took a step closer and said, "He is your son. You and Lucia have three wonderful sons, Tito. Remember? You have Mario and his lovely wife, Elena, and Lucio and his wife, Nunzia, and don't forget your wonderful grandchildren . . . ."

His frenzied glare shifted to me and the gun was in my face, as he screamed, "These worthless pigs raped my granddaughter. Look at her."

He stepped towards me as he said, "You tell me, Dani, would you let him – them – live if your daughter had been raped?"

I didn't have an answer. I was sorry I had said the word grandchildren and, no, I could not tell him I would let anyone live if they raped my daughter. I did not answer him. I couldn't.

Enrico tried to move closer but Tito turned to face him and said, "Stay where you are, Moravia."

The gun was uncomfortably close to my body. I gave a desperate look that Enrico understood immediately. He backed off with his arms in the air.

"Tito, I understand how you feel. We can get help . . . ."

Tito interrupted Enrico before he could complete the sentence and said, "I do not need help."

"For Fabio, for Angelina and for you, Tito . . . ."

With a violent shove, which propelled me toward Enrico's stalwart form, Tito interrupted Enrico's sentence and shouted, "I will shoot you, too, Inspector."

Enrico caught me and held me close. I looked up at him hoping for some sign of reassurance. I did not get one. I saw pain on his face. He understood the impossible anguish that had driven this man to this point in his life. We both understood because we had been family friends of the Scarlattis for years.

We heard the police sirens approaching and without a word between us we knew that the arrival of uniformed policemen could be the trigger that would set Tito off.

I stepped a few feet closer to Tito and quietly said, "Tito, the police are here. Please give me the gun and everything will be fine."

I would have preferred a defiant look and verbal response from him because this would have reassured me that he was still consciously aware of the concept of right and wrong. Yanking his son off of the ground Tito put the gun to Fabio's temple. Tito's hand started to shake. I hoped it was from sadness, but from the glint in his eyes, I knew that it was uncontrollable fury. I closed my eyes in anticipation of hearing the gun being fired. I knew that I would not be able to bear seeing my dear friend kill his own son.

Instead of the expected gunshot, I heard Tito rant at his son, "We gave you everything you wanted. You were our baby. You were . . . ."

Fabio meekly interrupted his father as he said, "I was Lucia's baby – mama's baby – never yours. I was never good enough. I could never compare to Mario or Lucio. Their children – especially Angelina, were the favored ones."

"You have ruined everyone's life – you are an ungrateful demon seed. You never looked like me! You are not my son!"

In that one short sentence, all became clear to me. In all the years that I had known the Scarlattis I had always marveled at how a father could treat his youngest child with such distain and contempt. I whispered to Enrico, "He doesn't think Fabio is his child."

"Papa, tu prego." Fabio pleaded "You are the only father I know. I don't understand how you can say I am not your son.

"You cannot be a son of mine. You hurt people. You hurt animals. You are evil." The gun had been lowered throughout the exchanges between father and son, but Tito raised it again and held it in front of Fabio's frightened visage. Once again I closed my eyes and waited for the gun to be fired.

Angelina moaned. I opened my eyes to see that she was gaining consciousness. I rushed over to her pulling off my jacket to drape over her naked body. I knelt down and said, "Sweetie, it's Dani. You are okay."

"Fabio, dov'é Fabio?" She looked around, but I could tell that she was having trouble focusing. She started to cry. I held her close and repeated, "You are okay."

"Angelina, stai bene?" Tito said as he let Fabio go and moved to Angelina's side. I watched as he placed the gun on the floor. He knelt down. As he brought her hands up to his lips and kissed each one, I gently loosened my hold on her and made room for Tito to get closer. Tears streamed down his face. "Why? Why do you do the drugs? Why do you act like a puttana?"

When Tito used the Roman slang word 'puttana,' which referenced prostitution, I suddenly had a picture that was one far more complicated than I had originally imagined. His questions to her must have meant that, by her own choice, she participated in these drug orgies and that she was, perhaps, the one that was using her uncle Fabio and not the other way around. As they whispered to each other, I took the gun.

I looked up at Enrico. He motioned with his head for me to move away from Tito and Angelina. I slowly got up, and we quietly walked toward the stairs. "Are your men waiting upstairs?" I asked as I handed him the gun.

"I told Massimo to bring Mario and Lucia." Enrico said. He sighed and then whispered, "But after hearing what Tito said I almost wish I hadn't. Do you think they know about Angelina?"

"Do you mean the 'puttana' issue?" I said.

"Exactly."

"I don't think so – what will I tell them?"

He whispered to me, "You will know what to say, darling. I need to get upstairs and stop my men from clomping down here and shooting up the place." He gave me a quick kiss on the cheek and quietly said, "I'm off. Try to keep him from doing anything dangerous."

The whispers between Tito and Angelina had continued through the exchange between Enrico and myself, so Tito had not realized that Enrico was no longer in the room.

For a few moments, I tried to formulate how I would broach the issue of Angelina to the Scarlatti family, but I didn't get a chance to pursue that thought because Tito rose from his crouched position near Angelina and went back over to Fabio. With the strength one would not expect from a man of his years, he hoisted his son off of the ground and dragged him over and dumped him next to the two cowering friends. "You are insects, parasites, vermin that do not deserve to live." He pointed a finger at the men and said, "Have your parents failed to do a favorable job for society by rearing such as yourselves or are you the failures?" He kicked each man in the chest. "You revolt me."

34

I heard voices coming from the upstairs entry foyer. I recognized Mario's and knew that he would be coming down the stairs in a few moments. I felt a hand on my shoulder. I looked at Enrico and whispered, "What can we do?"

Right after I said this, I watched in horror as Tito got a grip on his son and dumped Fabio on top of Angelina, as if he were a rag doll. "Here, Angelina, here is your Fabio." The look of disgust on his face was frightening.

Enrico placed the gun I had retrieved in my hand and walked toward Tito. "You are justifiably angry, Tito, but these young people are . . . ."

Before he could finish speaking Lucia Scarlatti flew down the stairs. "Tito, mio amore." She wrapped her arms around Tito's shoulders, effectively keeping him from moving. This only stopped him for a few moments. With a surge of angry power he flung her off and stared at her. "Lucia, you must not be here. You must not see the Scarlatti shame. You must leave."

Mario moved slowly to stand by his mother. He put an arm around Lucia and said, "Mother, father must resolve this tragedy in his own way."

"Cosa? Are you crazy?" She looked to Mario and then turned to look at Enrico and said, "Inspector, you must stop this."

As I watched the drama, I realized that Tito had not heard what Lucia or for that matter Mario or Enrico had said. With the force of the demon, he made sure Fabio stayed on top of the Angelina. "I can rid the Scarlatti family of shame permanently with one bullet." He raised a gun.

I gasped in horror. "Oh, God, Enrico, he had another gun – he's going to shoot both of them."

"God damn it – the Signora forgot to tell me that Tito took more than one gun."

Angelina hugged Fabio. She sobbed and said, "Please, grandfather, we are sorry. We . . . ."

"Silence. You were always my angel. You are a whore – a worthless whore." He shouted at her before she could say more.

35

Tito clicked the hammer and aimed at the two of them

Turning my head I closed my eyes.

The gun's report was deafening. I opened my eyes as Tito toppled to the floor. Suddenly I realized he had shot himself.

Lucia and Mario rushed over to him.

Enrico yelled to his men and rushed over to Tito. Within moments a doctor was at Tito's side. Enrico moved out of the way. Emergency medics with a stretcher came down the stairs followed by several policemen.

"You already had them here – the ambulance and medical staff! Enrico, you are a genius," I said as I hugged him.

"Thank you, darling. I knew when you got that phone call that we had a potential emergency on our hands. If I can't do something brilliant once in awhile what good am I?" As the attending medical workers looked Tito over, I waited for a sign that he wasn't dead. Lucia sobbed and held Tito's hand as they carried him away. I looked over and saw that Mario had wrapped Angelina in a cover and whispered to her while paramedics checked her over. Police officers stood by as Fabio and his friends grappled for clothing. I was sure that Enrico would share the details of their fates with me later.

As we followed everyone upstairs, a plain clothed policeman came up and said, "Sir, I overheard the doctor tell the Signora that Signore Scarlatti shot himself in the abdomen. The doctor believes that he will survive."

We walked out of the house and watched as the ambulances and police cars left. I turned and said, "Is this what all your days are like?"

"Wait a moment. Why are you asking what my days are like? You know what my days are like. Remember that you invited me for a relaxing lunch. I was not the one who involved us in the Scarlatti drama."

"Oh, details. Yes, I do know what your days are like. I guess my question is do all your cases deal with so much insanity?"

"No. I deal with people who are normal criminals – few are insane." He hugged me and smiled. "What, no snide remarks – no come back comment?"

"Weren't you the one who was gauging my life by the degree of insanity in which I get involved? May I ask how you decide to base your observations – is it on a daily, weekly or monthly measurement – is it coming from a 360-degree full circle? I need to know what the standard is by which all this is to be calculated."

"Oh, dear God, save me from this woman."

I tried to speak again, but he shut me up with a kiss. There was no discussion for several minutes. I decided not to let the discourse die, so I said, "I can't believe you ever used the word insanity when referring to me, my dearest Enrico."

"Of course, you were right. I suspect I should have never said that your insanity was demonstrated by degree – I should've said that you, your friends and family are all suffering from various stages of acute insanity – period, and cannot be measured by degree or any other way."

"I know you are trying to be glib to help me through what happened here. But in all seriousness what happened with Tito Scarlatti and the tragedy with how the children turned out . . . is – well – you know."

"Don't cry, darling Dani." Enrico said as he kissed my tears away. "They will all get help. I promise," Enrico said as he held me close and caressed my long blonde hair. After several pleasant moments in his strong arms he said, "Dani, the next time you invite me for Sunday lunch and relaxation I would appreciate it if we could do something else for excitement if you get my meaning."

"I smiled, kissed him and tugged on his arm as I said, "Come on, let's go back to my place for a swim and – well – you know."

SALAD OIL CAN GET YOU INTO HEAVEN
by Mary Ann Hutchison

I stood in the tiny kitchen, arms wrapped tightly around the sobbing gray-haired woman.

The soft sshh-ing of rubber wheels behind us indicated the Medical Examiner's gurney had come through the front door into the living room, and was traveling a hallway's well-worn linoleum toward the last room on its left. At the sound, the grieving mother sobbed harder, burrowing her head deeper into my left shoulder.

A blue-uniformed police officer leaning against the cracked green ceramic-tiled kitchen sink, smiled at me, then mouthed the words, "She didn't see." I winked in grateful acknowledgement.

While we waited for the gurney to make its return trip to the black van standing outside the small slump-block home on an early May morning, my eyes toured the kitchen. The counters held a few bags of groceries; cardboard boxes marked "cocina" (kitchen) were piled on the floor in front of cupboard doors. Guess they were unpacking when it happened.

A quick scurrying motion on the back wall of the sink caught my attention. Small gray-brown insects rushed up and down the wall, like micro autos on a freeway.

Well, if this isn't a kick in the head. Thank you, Lord. Just what she doesn't need. Isn't it enough that her dead son will be rumbling on a cart behind us in a minute? Now you throw in cockroaches?

I berated myself for yelling at God, and then for the self-doubt that was building in me. Did you do everything right? You're no priest. There were no how-to rules on Last Rites in the Catholic Catechism classes you took thirty-two years ago.

First thing in the morning, I'm calling the church and talking to a priest. Maybe I'll have to go to confession or . . . .

My thoughts broke as the police officer gently turned the grieving mother and me 180 degrees so that I now faced the living room; the distraught mother faced the kitchen sink. Had he not repositioned us, her last memory of her youngest son might have been his body, encased in a black zippered bag, leaving home for the last time. To this day, I love that man for his simple act of kindness extended to a heartbroken mother.

I whispered my thanks to the officer. Death was still present in the house. Speaking in normal tones seemed somehow sacrilegious.

The teary-eyed tiny mother stood back from my embrace, saying, "Gracias, señora."

I mumbled, "God bless you," as I gave her one last hug.

"Vaya con Dios," she said.

"Y tú. You also," I replied.

The officer who had been in the kitchen with us spoke briefly to three other officers who were also gathered in the living room.

"We're Code Four here. Let's go."

He turned to the two regular members of the Victim-Witness* Team seated in the living room.

"Thanks as usual for your help." He looked at me, "I didn't catch your name. Are you training for the program?"

"It's Mary Ann, and no, I'm just on ride-along tonight."

"Nothing like a baptism by fire," he commented.

The two volunteers (I'll call them Jane and Ellie; not their real names) beckoned to me, and we went outside and watched, along with a group of curious neighbors, as the Medical Examiner's men hoisted the gurney into the van.

"Okay, ladies," said Jane. "Let's call it a day."

The three of us headed back to the station to drop off the vehicle and the walkie-talkies provided to the V-W Teams by Pima County, Arizona, and write up our reports.

It was 4:30 a.m. and our tour of duty was finished. I was exhausted. It had been a very long Friday night for me. I'd left my job as courtroom clerk for the Pima County Superior Court at 5:00 p.m., and met with Jane and Ellie at the Tucson Police Department's Main Station at 6:00.

We had picked up the vehicle allotted to the Victim-Witness Program and a walkie-talkie and headed into an early spring evening to lend our assistance wherever it would be needed.*

As we drove back to the Police Department to turn in our reports, pick up our cars, and say good-bye, I asked, "Is it always like this?"

"Always like what?" Jane responded.

"Well, at first it was kind of boring. Seven o'clock on a Friday night, just sitting in Denny's having coffee, talking and listening to the walkie-talkie. Then, we had the wandering Alzheimer's patient call and the drive-the-drunk-home call. Each of them called for a different amount of knowledge and compassion, and took more time than I would have imagined. I really learned a lot. Then, back to Denny's, more coffee, a sandwich, sitting and waiting and just as we were getting ready to call it a night, this happens."

Ellie explained, "Sometimes, it is just plain boring. Sometimes, but not often, nothing much goes on. We call that a good night. And sometimes it's like tonight. We were coasting and then up pops death. Or, a guy beats the crap out of his wife, or there's a rape or a murder or an auto accident, and we're called on to assist the victims or their families."

"How do you deal with your emotions? I mean you two seem calm, cool and collected. I feel numb right now. I can't believe I did what I did."

"Do you really think we're as calm as you think we are?" asked Jane.

"I'm getting that impression."

She continued, "Never trust first impressions. Tonight, a young man died during an epileptic seizure. His family just moved here from up state and they don't have a parish priest nearby to help them. They don't speak much English, have no family near and distrust the system and strangers.

"Right now, I feel a lump in my throat and an ache in my heart for parents whose son died in a house that wasn't their home yet, in a strange town, without the comfort of their church. When I get home, I'll take a hot shower, cry and then go on with my life. Until then, I'll just bottle it up and finish my report, laugh and joke with the guys at the station and head home."

"Why do you do this every week? Put yourself on an emotional roller coaster, I mean," I said.

"How do you feel right now?" Jane asked.

"Half of me is a mess. I want to curl up in a ball and cry for all the reasons you gave, and maybe a few more. But then, the other half of me feels as if I made a difference to a family I'll never see again. I feel pretty damned good."

Ellie answered, "And that's why we do this every week. Because we make a difference in people's lives by remaining calm, having answers for their questions or finding the answers, or listening to their fears, or anger. We can't solve all their problems, but hopefully we cushion some of the blows just by being there, and freeing up law enforcement so they can get back on the street."

Ellie parked the vehicle in a spot marked "Reserved for Victim-Witness" in back of the police station. She and Jane turned sideways in their seats, and looked back at me. They reminded me of bookends.

"How do you think you appeared to the mother you were comforting?" Ellie asked.

"I tried to look calm and cool. I hope I didn't look like I felt."

"How was that?"

"Scared to death."

They chorused, "Why?"

"Okay. Here goes. When the first cop asked if any of the three of us were Catholic, I answered yes, without thinking about why he was asking that question. When he said the parents were adamant — they were not going to release their son's body to the Medical Examiner without his first receiving Last Rites, I still didn't realize what he wanted me to do. Then, I finally got it. I guess he thinks that all Catholics know how to give that sacrament."

"You mean you don't," asked Jane?

"Nope. I was born and raised Catholic, but I don't go to church every Sunday anymore. Just on the big holidays, or maybe to light a candle and say a special prayer now and then."

"Then why didn't you say that you didn't know?" Ellie said.

"Geez, I don't know. I saw the stricken looks on the parents' faces; saw everyone standing around waiting. Something told me that if I didn't do it, there could be an awful scene if the M.E.'s men tried to take the body without the parents' consent, so I just did it."

"Lady, that took guts," said Jane.

"I don't know if it took guts or not. You don't know the half of it. When the officer told me which room the son was in I got a chill. When I looked down the hallway, it seemed twice as long as it actually was and really dark, except for a light shining out of the last room on the left. I felt like I was a child again, afraid of the dark and in a Stephen King movie. But that wasn't the worst."

Ellie asked quietly, "What was?"

I couldn't help but laugh. "Oh, God, you are going to think I've gone around the bend. I mean it's funny now, but it wasn't then."

"For Lord's sake, spill it," Ellie shouted excitedly.

"Okay, here goes. As I walked down the hall, I remembered reading somewhere that when bodies go into rigor mortis, or maybe it was when they were coming out of rigor, I don't remember which, anyhow, the body would sit upright. Or that the body expelled gases and the dead seemed to sigh. I knew that if that happened, I'd wet my pants."

The three of us couldn't hold back the laughter. For a moment, laughing covered the sorrow we needed to bury.

When the laughter subsided, Jane said, "Go on."

"I only walked a few feet into the room when I saw this young man, boy, really, lying in a twin bed, a few feet from the doorway, in a dress-shirt and pants, with his arms folded onto his chest in that classic pose you've seen in the movies. He looked as if he was sleeping. I said a small prayer for help, said other prayers for Benny's soul, made the sign of the Cross and came back into the living room. And that was that. Except for trying to comfort his mom."

They were quiet for a minute or two, then Ellie said, "Would you write this up for our newsletter? It's really an interesting story."

I thought for a few minutes before answering. "Would you be disappointed with me if I didn't? If anyone had told me that I'd ever be giving Last Rites, I would have told them they were out of their ever-lovin' mind. Right now, it seems like bragging. I don't want to do that. It was such a personal moment. I'd rather keep it to myself."

"Are you sure," Jane asked?

"I am. I don't think I did anything special. Really. It was just something that needed to be done."

"Okay then. When you write your report, just omit those parts you want to keep personal."

But when I got home, I didn't go to bed right away. I waited until eight, phoned the church and asked for the priest on duty. It took him a few moments to get to the phone, and while I waited, I again was filled with self-doubt. What if I did everything wrong. What would that poor mother think if she ever found out? Was I going to hell? More importantly, was Benny going to hell?

When the priest picked up the phone, I blurted out my story.

"You say that it happened at four this morning?" he asked.

"Around there, yes, father. Was it okay? Is Benny — will he get into heaven in good shape?"

"You did just fine. You might not have used the exact words, but you chose the right prayers, asked Jesus to forgive his transgressions and accept him as a child of the Lord."

"Father, you don't know how good that makes me feel. I wasn't sure if he and I were both going to hell."

Laughing, he added, "You only missed one thing."

"What was that?"

"You could have anointed his forehead with oil, making the sign of the Cross."

"But I didn't have any Holy oil."

"Salad oil would have been okay."

"Father, are you joking?

"No, child. I'm not. In special circumstances, salad oil would have worked just fine."

"I'll be darned. Thanks for that information, just in case I have to do that again. God I hope not. I feel so much better."

"God Bless you."

"Thank you, Father. You, too."

Before falling asleep, I grinned. Crisco. Who knew?

*In 1975 the Pima County Attorney's Victim Witness Program (now Victim Services) was the first in the country to provide comprehensive assistance to victims of crimes. At that time, two volunteers would only be available on Friday and Saturday nights to render on-scene assistance to law enforcement agencies.

Currently, there is a staff of 25 paid and 120 volunteers who are on call 24 hours a day, seven days a week. Recently, the Arizona Constitution was amended to guarantee that a victim will be treated with dignity and respect. Victims have the right to be present at all court proceedings, the right to express opinions to the court and the right to confer with the prosecutor regarding the disposition of the case. They have the right to know of the defendant's release status. Victim Services, in conjunction with the prosecutors in the office, ensure these rights are enforced.

The Victim Services staff and volunteers have been called upon to work with the victims of the September 11th Terrorist attacks, the Oklahoma City bombing of the federal building, victims of the war and genocide in Bosnia and other local and national tragedies. Victim Services makes more than 16,000 victim contacts each year and helps more than 5,000 people at crisis scenes.

SEA 'SCAPES
by Ashleen O'Gaea

He expected to walk straight out through the surf to the deeper waves. The sand was supposed to slope away, gently at first and then so steeply he couldn't change his mind. He anticipated suffering a little shock and panic when his head went under and his last saved breath went out.

Instead, he stumbled into a sand bar.

"Damn! The epithet bubbled out into water not quite as deep as he was tall.

As he stood there, the water lapping his face and diluting his resolve, he noticed fluttering around his feet. Please, not a shark. God, were those teeth sinking into his legs? He took a breath and ducked his face under to look.

She had not expected to hit the sand bar either.

She'd been swimming fast, not paying much attention to her depth, and she'd hit hard. She thought at first that she'd managed to beach herself, but when she lifted her head, there was no air to assail her gills.

"Bait and hooks!"

Then she noticed a pair of feet. She touched them; they were solid as a tail, and she pulled her hand back, startled. Remembering she had nothing to lose, she patted to be sure there were legs above the feet. Then she dug her nails into the pale, skinny things and hauled herself upward to see what had come between her and the beach.

It took them both a moment to recover from the collision of their foreheads.

Their eyes met as both heads broke the surface. They blinked at each other, the dignity of their momentous shared discovery diminished

45

somewhat by the rapidly swelling red bumps, his spitting of sea water, and her blowing of air.

"Um," he said.

"Merra." She patted her chest. "Merra."

"Ron," he said. "My name is Ron. You, um, seem to be a mermaid."

"Merra," she corrected him again. "You seem to be a human."

He couldn't help noticing that she spoke English, and in his voice. It unnerved him. He wondered briefly if she had come to save him, like he'd heard dolphins sometimes saved drowning sailors.

"I don't want to be saved," he told her.

"Neither do I."

In equal surprise, they recognized their identical intentions.

"But why would you want to – ?" They spoke in unison and then laughed nervously.

"But you have so much to live for!" Again, and this time in harmony, which unnerved them both.

"There's nothing – " They laughed again, making their discomfiture graceful, spitting the gentle swells out of their mouths like old friends sharing sunflower seeds or brine shrimp.

"Why do you sound like me?"

"Yours is the only voice I've ever heard."

"You're the only mermaid I've ever met."

"I've never seen a live human before."

"I didn't mean for you to see me alive," he said, as if he were excusing to his mother last weekend's pizza box still open on the coffee table.

"You're nice, alive." He had never heard this from his mother.

"Am I?" He looked into Merra's eyes and saw that one was green and one was blue. His were brown. "I'm delighted that you're real."

"Are you?"

"Perhaps," he said, gurgling slightly as a small wave broke over his nose, "we should reconsider."

"Perhaps," she agreed, and coughed as the foam tickled her gills.

"We could meet here again, in, say, a month's time."

"What's a month?

For the first time in years, he knew immediately how to explain what he meant. "A moon cycle."

"Alright," she said. "Can you give me a push?"

She lowered herself back into the water and turned away from him. He took a deep breath and bent down. He wasn't sure where to push her from; she put her arms by her sides and wiggled her hands to show him.

He put the heels of his palms against hers and shoved her off the sand bar. She disappeared before she swam very far from him, but there were ripples in the water for longer.

He stood up and walked back toward the beach, hoping his clothes were still where he'd left them.

LORCAN AND THE WITCH
by Jude Johnson

Cries of "Thief! Thief! Grievous larceny!" rang across the meadow, startling blackbirds into flight in one big cloud from the trees. A short little man with wiry red hair waved stubby arms over his head and ran in circles as he yelled his alarm.

The young unicorn watched from her spot by the buttercups, calmly chewing sweet grass until the little man tripped over a chipmunk hole and fell, still growling and muttering. She ripped another mouthful of grass to munch before she moseyed over to tilt her head and look at him. "Whassa matta you?"

A rotten potato nose dominated a book-squashed face. Two fuzzy red caterpillars perched over beady black eyes. "I've been robbed, you silly horse! Someone stole me pot o'gold!"

"Notta horse. Yoo-nee-corn," she said, spattering wet bits of chewed green. "See? Horn." She lowered her head for him to see the single six-inch spike growing out of the middle of her forehead. "Not growed yet. Whadder you?"

"Are ya daft? I'm a leprechaun o'course!" He scrambled to his feet to stand. The top of his head barely reached the young unicorn's shoulder. Dressed in green knickers and short jacket, he repositioned his green top hat that sported a buckle just like the ones on his muddy shoes. "I make the rainbows you see after the rain from that pot. How am I to do me job without it, I ask you?"

The unicorn blinked her large sapphire eyes very slowly. "Dunno. Dunno how you make 'em in the first place. You 'kay—whassa name?"

"Lorcan the Leprechaun." He looked around, scowling the red caterpillars into a unibrow. "I'll bet I know who took it."

"Mmkay." The unicorn turned to leave.

"No ya don't! Come back here! I need a ride to the deepest, darkest part o'the forest. Take me to that nasty old witch's house."

"Ask nice. And she neither nasty nor old." The unicorn lifted her head high and tossed her mane. Shimmering rainbows reflected from those pearly tresses. "You got pretty candy? Red and white crunchy?"

"What, you think I'm Santy Claus handin' out candy canes? Look here, silly, I'm a leprechaun!" He reached into his pocket and threw a handful of four-leaf clovers into the air.

The unicorn's eyes opened wide and she pranced with excitement. "Mucky Karms!"

"What?"

"Mucky Karms—magically dee-lish-us." The unicorn licked her lips and nodded.

"Like, 'Always after me lucky charms?' No, no, that's me stoopid cousin, Lucky. He gets all the fame and I do all the work. I'm Lorcan. I have real four-leaf clovers, none o'that marshy-mallowy stuff. Sticks to me teeth and gives me the foulest winds."

The unicorn pouted. "No Mucky Karms? No ride."

Lorcan opened his mouth to speak, then stopped. A sly smile spread across his face. "Sure and I'll ask Lucky ta give you all the mucky karms—I mean Lucky Charms—you could want. But you have to take me to the deepest, darkest part o'the forest first."

The unicorn thought a moment and nodded.

"Good! Now just go over there by that stoomp fer me to get on."

"What?"

"The stoomp! The stoomp, you goofy horse!" Lorcan pointed across the meadow. "Right there, where the tree broke and fell."

"Oh! You mean the stump. You talk funny."

"I talk funny?" Lorcan scrarmbled up onto the tree stump. "You're the one what calls 'em 'Mucky Karms.'"

He jumped onto the unicorn's soft white back and grabbed onto a fistful of sparkly mane. He jerked his heels back with great gusto. "Now giddyup!"

"Ow! Don't kick!"

49

"Then get movin'! Lord knows what that old witch is doin' with me pot o'gold! Probably spent it on something stoopid like a Cad-a-lack."

The unicorn turned her head back to look at him. "Why are you so mean? Need a nap."

"No, I don't." Lorcan waved a grimy hand forward. "Let's go."

She trotted across the meadow and through the trees with a pretty prancing gait. Lorcan bounced uncomfortably up and down on his bum but he grit his teeth and stayed quiet, thinking that if he complained, she'd hop like a bunny.

Sunlight peeked through the leaves, dappling the path ahead—but only for the first little while. As they continued, the trees grew closer together, thick with fat leaves and moss. Soon it was very gloomy.

"Hey! Watch where you're goin'!" Lorcan ducked as a low branch whipped his hat from his head. He barely caught it, hauling hard on a fistful of mane as he nearly fell off the unicorn's back.

"Ow! Don't pull my mane!"

"And you don't hafta run under the lowest branches you can find!

The unicorn blew a raspberry sound from her lips. "I no make the path. You watch out for branches—they no bother me."

Suddenly the forest opened into an area carpeted with pine needles and brown leaves. But unlike the other meadow, there wasn't much sunlight. Interlocking tree branches wove a dark dome above a small brown house across the way. Blue smoke wafted up from a rusty-red chimney poking up through a yellow thatched roof. A dark green hedge surrounded the dwelling, broken only by a small black gate.

"We're here," the unicorn snorted. "Get off!" She turned and stretched her neck around to nip Lorcan's jacket with her teeth. She dragged him from her back, dumping him unceremoniously on his butt in front of the gate. "Mucky Karms now?"

"Hold yer self." Lorcan stood and brushed his pants free of leaves, then settled his hat more firmly. "Get it? I said 'hold yer self' 'cause you're a horse. Hold yer horses—oh, never mind. I told ya my cousin, Lucky, has Lucky Charms, not me. But thanks for the ride—sucker!"

He reached for the gate latch. It opened with a loud, raspy, long creak.

A weird sort of wailing whinny echoed around the dark clearing below the trees. Lorcan turned. The unicorn stood crying, her neck stretched forward, snot bubbling from her nostrils, and her fat lower lip all a-tremble. Huge tears rolled from her blue eyes and splashed into a rapidly filling bowl of cupped leaves.

"Stop that nonsense, you whiny beast!" Lorcan huffed with his hands on his hips.

"What have you done to Gwynne?" A commanding voice rang sharply from within the house. "You have to be one wicked slice of nasty to make a unicorn cry."

Lorcan gulped. That must be the mean old witch! He couldn't see anyone beyond the shadowed doorway and he quivered—just a bit—with fear.

But then he thought about his missing pot o'gold and greed set his jaw. "Come out here! I wanna talk to you."

Shadows hugged the house beneath the edges of the thatched eaves. Lorcan squinted as the gloom shifted and a beautiful lady dressed in flowing silver robes stepped forward.

Her pearly white hair glimmered with iridescence like the unicorn's even in the dimness of the forest, flowing over her shoulders. She moved across the threshold with grace. Her oval face carried not a wrinkle. But her large, dark-lashed eyes were grey storm clouds that flashed with anger.

Lorcan gulped. "Where's that mean old witch—the one what stole my pot o'gold? You send her out here!"

"I'm the only witch in this part of the forest," the lady said in a rich mellow voice. "And I ask you again, what did you do to Gwynne to make her sob like that?"

The unicorn blubbered, "Waaah! He mean, Rhian! (sob) He promised (snort) Mucky Karms but (snork) nooooo! Waaah-hah!"

The witch pursed her lips and shook her head. "Ooh, that's a big, bad no-no, lying to a unicorn."

"So's stealing!" Lorcan planted his fists on his hips. "You stole me pot o'gold! I can see it right there on that table in yer house!"

"Best be careful what words you throw at me, Lorcan the Leprechaun. Oh yes," the witch nodded, "I know who you are. And as far as 'stealing' your pot, I found a nice little black cauldron sitting unattended out in the meadow."

"Was not!" Lorcan stomped his foot. "It was hidden behind the stoomp!"

"The what?"

"The stoomp, the stoomp!" Lorcan rolled his eyes and threw his hands up. "Where the tree fell!"

"You mean a stump. And no, it sat right out in the open. Leaving it without so much as a label on it is pretty silly. If it is yours, describe the insides."

He squinted at her. "Is this a trick? Everyone knows it's black and full o'gold. What would you want it for but to take it all and buy something stoopid like a Cad-a-lack!"

To Lorcan's surprise, the witch threw her head back and laughed. "A 'Cad-a-lack?' What would I want with that? And what would I want with your gold?" She turned and gestured to the table barely visible inside her house. "It's all right there. I only wanted the cauldron. It's the perfect size to wash my panties in."

"WHAT?" Lorcan sucked in his breath so hard it hurt his chest. "Are ye daft, woman? I use that pot ta make rainbows! You can't be washin' panties in it! Why, the rainbows will be ruined for sure! I can just see it: red, yellow, orange—and a big brown skidmark right in the middle!"

"Don't be silly." The witch shook her head. "Why don't you take your gold and go buy another pot?"

Lorcan stomped his feet in place with each word. "No, no, no, no! That's the rainbow pot and nothing else will do. Give it back. I'll have to scrub the insides with Clorox and fade the rainbows, but at least they won't have big brown skidmarks arching across the sky!"

The witch crossed her arms. "Well, I'm not convinced this was yours to begin with. You can go get a good sturdy replacement at The Kitchen Cauldron Shoppe. And don't forget to bring Gwynne some Lucky Charms. You owe her payment for bringing you."

"Mmfft!" Lorcan fumed. "Gimme mah gold."

She smiled. "You have money in your pockets, Lorcan. No leprechaun is ever without a coin or two."

Lorcan sniffed loudly and stomped off behind the witch's cottage. He could still hear the unicorn's occasional sob but he didn't care. He grumbled along, "Stoopid horse," and "Why should I have to buy that witch a pot when she took mine? I'll show her!"

It wasn't long before he came to the edge of the forest, surprisingly close to a village. The Kitchen Cauldon Shoppe, Shillelaghs R Us, Patti O'Furniture, and CheepyMart sat at the corners of the village green.

Lorcan marched straight past The Kitchen Cauldron Shoppe across the green to CheepyMart. He found a tin pot that looked as though it had been used as a ball in a goat's rugby game. A devious twinkle lit his eyes when he paid for it with leprechaun gold, knowing full well the coin would disappear within the hour.

He returned to the witch's cottage and pounded on the door. "Here," he said and held the pot out when she opened it.

Her right brow arched so high it disappeared beneath the bangs of her pearly white hair. "I'm surprised you chose so poorly, Lorcan. After all, this is your replacement."

Lorcan pulled the pot away and held it to his chest. "Well then, I'll keep it. At least this one hasn't had stinky panties in it! Now gimme back me gold. Those stoopid humans expect to find a pot o'gold at the end of the rainbow." He sneered with a nasty chuckle. "But what they don't know is, I charm the pot to move to the opposite end they go to. No human will ever find it. Ever."

"Did you get Gwynne her treat?"

"No." Lorcan stuck his jaw forward. "I didn't see me cousin around."

The witch shook her head sadly at him. "Do you still have four-leaf clovers in your pockets?"

"Yes..." He looked sideways at her.

"Put some into the pot."

He did as she asked and sprinkled a paltry few wilted clover leaves into the bottom.

"You're a very sad being, Lorcan. You've never learned to share, or care for anyone but yourself." The witch tapped the metal with her knobby gnarled wooden wand with a clunk and said:

Let Mucky Karms fill this pot
Not just a little but a lot.

Suddenly the clovers popped and multiplied like popcorn into brightly colored bits of cereal and marshmallow.

"Pour them into my apron."

Lorcan did as he was instructed. The witch turned and went into her cottage for the briefest of moments. When she returned, she said, "Let's see that pot again."

Lorcan slowly held it out, but kept a tight grip on the handles.

She opened her apron and shiny leprechaun gold cascaded and clattered into the battered CheepyMart tin as she chanted:

Once this pot is hidden from view,
So shall it stay from anyone who
Seeks the gold inside with greed,
For as you give, so you receive.

"Hah! And about time!" Lorcan snatched it back and turned away. "You'll never steal from me again!" he yelled over his shoulder, stomping back down the path toward the sunny meadow.

The unicorn poked her head out of the cottage, munching slowly. "Meany gone?"

"Yes, Gwynne. And I don't think he'll bother us again."

"You charmed the gold, dincha Rhian?"

"Yep. Once hidden, no one will ever, ever find it—including him."

They laughed and went inside to have more Magically Delicious Mucky Karms.

DOUBTING THOMAS
by Carol Costa

The first time she saw the storefront mission in Fairmont, West Virginia, Fay Perry wanted to take back the wedding vows she had just made and run for her life. She had promised to stand by Joe for better or worse, for richer or poorer, and as she gazed around at the peeling paint, the battered table and chairs and the cracked windowpanes, it was apparent that she was already being put to the test.

"It isn't much, honey," Joe told her quickly. "But I know you. In a few days, you'll have this place looking great."

It was 1937, the country was in the midst of a depression and about to be dragged into the war that was raging in Europe.

Fay looked at her handsome new husband. Joe Perry was already considered a miracle worker. As a fundraiser, he had traveled across the country coaxing nickels and dimes into the collection plates that supported the Church's mission programs. People said he could charm the angels right out of their wings.

Now he had been given his toughest assignment yet, to establish this mission in the tiny town of Fairmont. As his wife, Fay had also accepted the challenge.

"I guess I'd better have a look at the kitchen and make a list of what we need there," Fay said with a weak smile.

Instantly, Joe was at her side, wrapping his strong arms around her. "You won't be sorry, Fay. I promise, we're going to have a good life here."

Outside, a man in splattered overalls was already painting the words, "Union Rescue Mission" on a sign over the front door. In an adjacent room, twelve metal cots with worn mattresses were waiting to be made with the linens donated by a local department store.

Before the paint was dry on the new sign, the beds were made and filled with needy men. As the months passed, there seemed to be a never-ending stream of people who had nowhere else to go.

Joe believed that most poor people just wanted a chance to work and be useful, so he developed programs that gave them the opportunity to earn their keep. While the majority stayed only a short time, there were a few who became a permanent part of the mission staff.

One of those who stayed was Oscar Witt, an apparent misfit of a man, strong in stature and simple of mind. One rainy morning, Fay found him standing in the front room of the mission where the services were held. He was turning around in a circle looking the place over. She greeted him as she did every newcomer, not realizing this lost soul dressed in a pair of faded overalls and a plaid shirt that just barely covered his large torso, would someday give new meaning to the words faith and friendship.

"Welcome," Fay said. "Would you like to sit down? I can get you a cup of coffee."

Oscar snatched the cap from his head revealing short, choppy patches of dark hair. "Oh, no ma'am," he replied. "I didn't come here for no handout. I'm lookin' for work is all."

"I'll get my husband," Fay said at once. "Please sit down."

A few minutes later, Joe found Oscar still standing in the same spot, twisting his cap nervously. "I'm Joe Perry. My wife tells me you're looking for work."

Oscar grabbed Joe's hand and shook it so hard, Joe nearly lost his balance. "Oscar Witt. Pleased to make your acquaintance, sir . . . eh . . . I mean brother."

Extracting his hand from Oscar's mighty grip, Joe explained what was expected of the men who lived at the mission. "We're expanding, and in the process of building more beds and cabinets. We can always use another pair of hands. Of course, you understand this is a mission. We can't pay wages, but we can give you room and board for your labor."

"That'll be fine, mister . . . eh . . . sir . . . eh . . . brother."

"Perry. Joe Perry. You'd better just call me Joe."

Oscar grinned revealing several spaces where teeth were supposed to be. "And you can call me Oscar. This sure is a swell place you got here. I like it. And I'll work real hard for my keep."

"I'm sure you will," Joe agreed.

That same day, just before evening services, Oscar approached Fay. He stood in front of her for a few seconds, shuffling his feet nervously. "Is something wrong?" Fay finally asked.

"Oh, no ma'am. It's just that I've got a favor to ask and I kinda hate doin' it so soon after gettin' here."

"You go ahead and ask," Fay replied. "We're all here to help each other."

"I was just hopin' I could write a letter to my mama . . . just to let her know where I am and all. I'm not too good at puttin' words on paper though, so I was hopin' you could help me a little."

"I'd be glad to," Fay promised. "We'll do it first thing tomorrow morning."

"Oh, boy, this is sure a good day for Oscar," he exclaimed. And so the letters to Oscar's mother who lived in Ohio began. The writing sessions were always the same.

"Dear Mama, I am fine. How are you?" Oscar dictated. Fay wrote down Oscar's words and looked up at him. Oscar smiled and said nothing else.

"What's next?" Fay prompted.

"Gee, Missus Purry, can't you just tell her how things are. How I'm working hard, and you know what to say."

"Oscar. It's your letter to your mother."

"I know, but Mama won't care, if you write it. Please, I promised I'd help Tom with the cleaning this morning."

"Okay," Fay would say reluctantly. "Go ahead. I'll think of something."

"And don't forget to tell her that I miss her and will be home to visit real soon," Oscar always said before he ran off.

Of course, the months turned into years, and Oscar never could go home to visit his mama. No matter how hard he worked at the mission, there was simply not enough money to pay for a train ticket to Ohio.

Oscar got along well with the rest of the mission's growing staff, which included Martha and Frances, two Bible teachers from New York. Joe had invited them to visit the mission for a week just to try out a program for the young people and the ladies never left.

One of Oscar's special friends at the mission was Little Joe, a Polish immigrant who charmed everyone with his accent and his personality. Little Joe always worked in the kitchen alongside Fay, and took his duties very seriously. One of his jobs was to clear the tables after meals, and as he was doing that one night, two newcomers to the mission got up and tried to help him.

"You, men, no touch dishes," Little Joe told them. "Is my job."

One of the men shrugged and put the dishes down, but the other, a tall, burly man ignored Little Joe's warning.

"Hey, mister," Little Joe shouted. "You no hear so good. Leave dishes for Little Joe."

"Who died and left you boss?" the man shouted back.

"I say stop, you stop. Me boss of kitchen when Missy not here. Is my job. You go outside."

The man laughed and picked up another stack of dishes. Feeling that his position of importance was being threatened, Little Joe rushed over to retrieve the dishes, but the larger man held the dishes over his head while Little Joe jumped up trying to reach them.

"Come on, little man, jump a little higher. Or maybe you should go into the kitchen and get a ladder," the bigger man taunted. Little Joe's face was red with anger and he continued to jump in the air trying to grab the dishes. His tormentor and a few others who were still in the dining room howled with laughter.

Then the man with the dishes felt a large, heavy hand on his shoulder. In a quiet voice, Oscar said. "If the game is over, I expect Little Joe would like to get on with his chores without no more trouble. Right, brother?"

"I was only trying to help," the man said defensively, as he handed the stack of dishes to Little Joe.

"No help me," Little Joe insisted. "My job. Missy say is my job."

The man shrugged and walked out. Little Joe looked up at his big friend, Oscar, wanting to express his gratitude, but not knowing how to put it into words.

"It's your job," Oscar said firmly. "And you do it real good."

That was the first time anyone at the mission saw a sterner side to Oscar. Other than his frequent letters to his mama, even Joe and Fay didn't know much about Oscar's background or what had brought the big gentle man to their doorstep.

Then an hour later, in the midst of the evening service, Oscar decided to tell all. Perhaps it was the confrontation in the dining room that brought the story out, or perhaps Oscar just felt it was time to confide in his friends.

He jumped to his feet, startling everyone in the room. "I want to testify," he shouted. Then he smiled and shifted his feet like he did during the letter writing sessions and looked at Joe for help.

"Just try to say what's in your heart, Oscar," Joe advised.

Oscar took a deep breath and tried to stand a little taller. "Before I came here, the only person who loved me was my mama, and I expect that's cause I'm her only son," Oscar said with no trace of a smile on his face or in his voice. "I was married one time and had two little children. I loved them, but they was so different from me. I guess they couldn't love me back the way I wanted them to."

Every eye in the room was on Oscar as he paused and took another deep breath. Then the rest of his story thundered through the gathering like the shock of a sudden hailstorm on a bright summer day.

"Anyway, my wife took up with another man, and I came home one day with a gun. I was going to kill them . . . shoot them dead. I didn't care about anything . . . or anyone. I was full of the devil himself, and I would have shot them full of holes, sure as potatoes have skins, only they saw me comin' and ran off before I got there. Took the children with 'em, and I ain't never seen any of 'em again."

Again Oscar paused, this time to look around at the stunned faces of the gathering. Then, he plunged ahead. "So anyway, I didn't shoot nobody . . . and later on, I was glad I didn't, but inside of me there was still that awful empty feelin'. I didn't belong to no one and no one belonged to me. I never thought about God or Jesus Christ. I just wandered around with that empty feelin', not gettin' any worse and not gettin' any better . . . but being here with all of you I feel somethin' inside me again . . . somethin' good, fillin' up all that empty space . . . and I know it's because I've been here living and working with you folks. Brother Purry . . . and Sister Purry didn't ask me no questions when I came here . . . just took me in . . . like I was a good Christian, same as them, and so now I am . . . and that's my testimony." Oscar looked at Joe for approval. "Is that all right, Brother Purry?"

"That was just fine, Oscar," Joe assured him. "We're pleased and proud to have you with us."

The following week, Fay gave birth to her first child, a girl named Janet. After a few days, Fay and the new baby were preparing to leave the hospital when a nurse came into the room.

"I'm sure glad to see you leave," the nurse said.

Fay was taken back by her remark. "Oh?"

"Oh, nothing against you," the nurse said quickly. "It's that big man who works at the mission. He's been here every few hours since you were admitted. We've all explained that you're not really sick, just resting after having a baby. He says okay, and goes away only to show up again, with a worried look and more questions about your welfare."

Fay didn't have to ask the man's name, she knew it was Oscar.

The next morning, Fay had a talk with Joe and some of the other staff members. "Oscar's birthday is next month," she told them. "I think we should plan a special surprise for him."

Everyone was more than happy to take part in Oscar's birthday celebration. The extra sacrifices they all made were rewarded by the look of sheer joy on Oscar's face when they presented him with a cake and presents.

"Blow out the candles, Oscar," Joe instructed. "If you get them all in one breath, your wish will come true."

The big man gulped in some air, then blew out the candles all at once. His friends applauded and Oscar grinned in triumph. "This is a mighty big cake," Oscar told them. "Enough for everyone, I expect."

"That's right," Fay replied. "But before we cut the cake, we have something else for you. Little Joe?"

Little Joe sprang forward and handed Oscar an envelope. Oscar opened it carefully and extracted its contents.

"A ticket? A ticket for the train?" he asked in wonder.

"Not just ticket," Little Joe cried. "Special ticket. You go to visit your mama, like you always say in letters and to us. You wish to see her, now you go."

A fearful look jumped into Oscar's eyes, and Fay quickly reassured him. "Now you're just going for a visit, mind you," she said firmly. "We expect you to come back to us."

Relief flooded Oscar's face and he smiled broadly. "Oh, boy, this is sure a good day for Oscar. I . . . I . . . I thank you very much."

Everyone applauded and cheered, and then Frances and Martha gave Oscar another present to open.

Oscar stared at it. "I never had a present wrapped up so beautiful before. Missus Purry, you help Oscar, please." Fay took the box and removed the lovely wrappings. Inside the box was a suit.

"You're always so helpful to us with the children," Martha explained. "So Frances and I got this suit at the secondhand store. We want you to look nice when you see your mama."

"We could only guess at the size," Frances added. "But if it needs alterations, we can do it for you."

Oscar lifted the suit from the box as if it were the crown jewels. His soft brown eyes filled with tears as he hugged the jacket to his chest. "Oh, boy," he exclaimed. "Cake and presents—what a good day for Oscar."

A few days later, Joe took Oscar to the train station. Oscar was dressed in his new suit and carried a rather nice leather suitcase.

"The train will be pulling in any minute," Joe told Oscar. "Now, you know what you're supposed to do. Give your ticket to the conductor and don't get off the train until he tells you. Your mama said she'd be waiting to pick you up in Columbus."

"I can't hardly wait to see my mama," Oscar said. "It's been such a long time. And when I get back, I'll work harder than ever to make up for all you done for me. Gee whiz, wait till Mama sees me all decked out in this new suit, carryin' this snazzy suitcase. She won't know it's me."

"Just remember to bring the suitcase back," Joe warned. "I don't mind letting you use it, but it's the only one I have. It was a gift from my parents and it's very special to me."

"Oh, I know that," Oscar said solemnly. "And you don't have to worry, Brother Purry. I promise I'll bring it back, safe and sound." As the train whistle sounded, Oscar took a step back. "You know, Brother Purry, all of a sudden, I'm happy and sad at the same time. I'm sure gonna' miss you and all my friends at the mission. You'll keep an eye on Little Joe so nobody tries to bully him?"

"Stop worrying." Joe laid a hand on the big man's shoulder. "Everything is going to be just fine. And when you get back with my suitcase, I'll be here to pick you up."

A week later, Fay walked into the mission office to find Joe sitting there with a worried look on his face. "What's wrong?" she asked immediately. Joe Perry didn't waste time worrying over trivial things.

"I went to the station to pick up Oscar, but he wasn't on the train."

Fay frowned and reached for the telephone. "We'd better see if we can call his mother."

Joe placed his hand over hers. "I already did that, honey. She says that a neighbor drove Oscar to the station in plenty of time for him to catch the train home."

"Oh, Joe, no. Your call must have her very worried."

"I suppose," Joe admitted. "But she told me a few things about Oscar, so it's possible he never meant to come back here."

"What things?"

"His mama told me that Oscar was AWOL from the army. They came to her house looking for him, just about the time he showed up here. She said she talked to him about it while he was there, and now she's afraid she might have frightened him into running off again."

"I can't believe that Oscar would run off. He was happy here."

Joe shook his head sadly. "It's like we've said before, Fay. Sometimes people choose to turn away from us, and there's nothing we can do about it."

Fay put her arms around her husband. "Oh, Joe, I know it hurts, but look at it this way. If Oscar is able to face the world on his own again, it's because we gave him something he needed for this journey."

"Well, I know one thing he's got that he didn't have before," Joe replied with a wry smile. "My nice leather suitcase."

Several weeks passed, with no word of Oscar. It wasn't the first time that someone had strayed from their fold, but Fay thought that Joe was taking Oscar's disappearance especially hard. He was convinced that Oscar had deliberately run off and become a drifter again. Fay didn't want to believe that Oscar could turn his back on the mission and all his friends there, but it seemed like the only logical explanation.

Life at the mission continued. With a new baby to take care of, Fay had limited her work in the kitchen to lunch and dinner preparations, leaving clean ups to Little Joe and some of the other staff members.

This particular afternoon, baby Janet was falling asleep in Fay's arms. As she gazed down at her daughter's perfect features, Fay was suddenly filled with doubts. What kind of life would this child have at the mission? There were no luxuries here, only long hours and hard work, and there were so many lost souls to tend. . . .

Fay's thoughts were abruptly interrupted as Little Joe burst into the room with his eyes popping, nearly knocking over a chair.

"What's wrong?" Fay whispered, alarmed by the sudden intrusion.

"Come quick, Missy! In the kitchen. Come quick."

Fay hurriedly placed the baby safely in her crib and ran after Little Joe who was sprinting back towards the kitchen at a fast pace.

In the kitchen, Fay found Martha and Frances huddled over a big dark shape just inside the back door. As she ran over to them the ladies stepped back and Fay realized the man collapsed on the floor like a bag of dirty laundry was Oscar. He was wearing his suit, which was filthy and tattered. His shoes were in shreds and blood was oozing from his swollen mangled feet.

"Go find Joe," Fay told Martha.

With the help of Frances and Little Joe, Fay managed to get Oscar into a bed and began bathing his wounded feet. A few minutes later, her husband came running into the room.

Despite his injuries, Oscar broke into a huge grin. "Howdy, Brother Purry," he said as Joe approached the bed.

"My Lord," Joe whispered. "When they told me you were back, I couldn't believe it. What happened to you?"

"I'm sorry I worried you all," Oscar told him. "I missed the train and it's a mighty long way from Ohio."

"He walked, Joe," Fay spoke softly, unable to keep the tears from her eyes or her voice. "All the way from Ohio. His feet are a mess, his shoes practically disintegrated."

"He says he missed the train, and got confused," Martha added.

"Oscar, why didn't you call us?" Joe asked, incredulously.

"I don't know your phone number, Brother Purry. All I knew was I promised to get back here with that suitcase you were kind enough to lend me, and I did. It's safe and sound, just like I promised."

"That's right," Fay agreed. "The suitcase is in wonderful shape."

Joe stared down at the big man on the bed and shook his head from side to side. "And once again, Doubting Thomas learns a lesson," Joe said.

"Who's he, Brother Purry?" Oscar asked. "Gosh, you probably got a lot of new men while I was gone."

"Yes, we did," Joe replied. "But not one of them could take your place."

"Oh, boy." The big man sighed. "This is sure a good day for Oscar." And with a contented smile on his lips, he closed his eyes and fell asleep.

Joe came over and put his arms around Fay. It reminded her of the first day she stepped foot in the Union Mission. She had been a "Doubting Thomas" then, and less than an hour ago, she had been worrying about Janet and how living at the mission would affect her. For Fay, Oscar's unexpected return was like a rainbow lighting up a rain soaked sky.

Life at the mission would never be easy, yet Oscar had risked everything to get back to it. For Fay, Oscar's incredible journey was a message of love and hope delivered just when she needed it most.

As for Oscar, when his feet healed, he kept his promise and worked harder than ever. He never left the Union Mission again, not even to visit his mama.

ALCHEMY IN THE ANDALUSIA
by D.H. Tremont

"Please, Mistress Ambriel, must you alter my memory?" Little Joshua cried as he hung on to my neck. "May I not retain the wisdom of how you were called to us by my father?" As he asked this question, he looked like a mere waif of seven or eight. His small size negated his commencement into the first phase of manhood. A glimmer of the personality of this precocious 13-year-old flickered into his sad brown eyes as he said, "Perhaps one day I shall need to use the incantations and spells he invoked. Please, I promise I will never reveal your secrets."

Our hug was a mutual expression of a deep love which we had shared these last few weeks. My affection for this delicate young boy was the very reason that I knew I must do that which he asked me not to do. "No, child, this knowledge you may not keep. It was never meant to be used." His visage was one of such dejection that I held him even closer as I explained, "Other wisdoms shall be yours."

"My father and my uncle knew of these wisdoms, why may I not?"

"This world is not a place where such wisdoms are to be known or shared."

"Mistress, please . . . ."

I silenced his protestation by gently touching his face, and I shook my head no as I said, "Joshua, your family is going to die to protect you. Your life must not be jeopardized." I gently released him. With relief, we settled on a wooden bench to rest. I did not tell him that I had erased the memories of his father and uncle to protect my secrets; as I knew that the persuasive tools of the inquisition would cause these secretive alchemists to reveal all to end the suffering.

"That cannot be. They cannot die. It is unjust. We were promised safety when we became conversos. Uncle told me of many who converted from Judaism to Christianity who have attained high positions in the church," he said as he got up and stood in front of me. He twirled a tendril of my long blonde hair in his fingers and looked at me for reassurance.

"Yes, Joshua, and these very conversos who have achieved these places in the ecclesiastical hierarchy are using their positions to be the most severe detractors of Judaism in order to get rid of their enemies and gain more wealth and power," I said as I lowered the hood on my coal black pallium.

"No, no, grandfather told me King Ferdinand's father had named as his court astronomer a Jewish man."

"Yes. His name was Abiathar Crescas, but the time of Jewish service to the crown, whether as a Jew or a converse, has passed, dear one. With the murder of the inquisitor, Pedro Arbires, public opinion turned against conversos. The influence of Jews in Aragonese administration or any other ended with that single act." I explained as I undid the metal clasp of the heavy cloak I wore. It fell off of my shoulders onto the bench. Mollified I realized that my long persimmon colored tunic and gathered skirt still afforded warmth against the dampness of the room. I removed Joshua's cape with a single motion and placed it next to me.

I watched as this heir to ancient techniques of mining, smelting and smithery, passed on by secret rites, walked around his family's alchemy laboratory. The furnace, which traditionally was blazing hot, stood cold and dark, leaving a lingering odor of burned wood and made the underground cellar workshop gloomy and cold. Two oil lamps gave shadowed illumination to the scene. On now dusty tables stood porcelain vessels, beakers, and glass vials holding elixirs with the names written in exquisite Latin script.

A large chart hung on the wall showing the serpent eating its tail. Joshua ran his hand over the huge Ouroboros with his fingers distractedly touching the words and symbols written in Latin and Arabic. The opposite wall displayed many charts and diagrams. Scents strange to me permeated the air; mephitic, actinic and rancid – perhaps the result of experiments left uncompleted. On the table in the middle of the room instruments of geometry and alchemy were strewn: various hourglasses, a compass, an assortment of spheres and different size scales.

To draw him out of his musings, I said, "You have a special destiny that you must fulfill. I am here to effectuate this goal."

"Then, Mistress Ambriel, if it is true that my family must die, do I not owe them and those who shall be part of my destiny, all of the wisdom that I have ascertained from you?"

"Joshua, your insight and wisdom are part of that which you are - part of the secret wisdoms your parents taught you before I came to help you."

"I have learned much from you. Would I not serve my destiny better if I remember all you have taught me? May I not keep these secrets also?"

"If I allow you to keep the secrets you have learned from me, and the magic spells your father uncovered and ill- advisedly used, then you will become a victim of the Inquisition as your parents already have."

Held down by heavy bricks, there lay a half opened parchment scroll with the symbol of the caduceus visible. Joshua moved a brick and looked at the scroll. He then walked over to where hundreds of rolled up scrolls lay side by side in diamond-shaped wooden holes recessed in the adjacent wall. "All the scrolls and manuscripts my father and uncle worked from . . . what will become of them?"

"They shall be sequestered in safety until such time that the knowledge within them can be used to enlighten mankind," I said as I got up and walked to stand near the young man. As he turned to look at me I touched the wall, sending the documents to a diverse parallel dimension which rendered all invisible: thus locking away the knowledge of how to summon me or others like me.

"Will I be the one to find these scrolls?" he said as he fingered the other scattered parchments on the table.

"If you are worthy and can use them to help mankind then you will find them," I answered as I tapped the table to dispatch the scrolls to perceived oblivion. With a wave of my hand, the charts and diagrams on the remaining walls became senseless colored ramblings.

"Shall I remember that which I gleaned from my father's teachings?"

I knelt down to look in his eyes and said, "Yes, child, you will recall most of it, as this is part of the secret that you had already possessed before I was summoned by your father."

"We are true conversos as so many of our faith had to become when the Inquisition began. We were promised . . . ."

I stood up as I placed two fingers over his Cupid bow lips to silence his protestations. He turned away and sat on a wooden stool and placed his elbows on the large wooden table and covered his eyes and sobbed. As he wiped his eyes he looked at me and said, "Will you tell me the tale, yet again, of the ethereal world where you have journeyed from and how my father with his magic summoning spell brought you to us?"

I laughed and gently touched his cheek and said, "No, my little lad, I will not tell you that story, yet again. I will tell you many things, my dear one, but not by words. I shall give to you wisdom through thought. I shall plant knowledge deep within your mind like the seeds of many life-giving plants. As you get older and exist within the turmoil of the world, you will remember that which you need. You will not recall that which you have learned from me as coming from me but as a body of knowledge that you will impart from your inner wisdom. You will have access to all the wisdom you need to know in order to fulfill your destiny."

"Truly?"

Without his conscious awareness, I touched his temples and planted within his subconscious all the secrets he would need and removed those he should not retain and said, "Truly."

"May I not journey with you to your special place? The one you spoke of in your tale?"

"No, Joshua. Your presence on this earth dimension is vital to the awakening process of man," I explained as I sat on a stool next to him.

"Is your home heaven?"

"All places are part of God and part of what you call heaven."

"I understand not – how do all places exist in heaven?"

"You are too young to understand but I promise you that as you become a man your wisdom will increase and you will know many things and share them with others."

"Will I travel and write great treatises?"

"You will do many things, and the world will know you as Paracelsus."

"Oh, tell me of my life..."

Before I could tell him of the wonders that his new life would bring, angry voices could be heard coming from several nearby alleyways. Seeking a place to hide, from the soldiers, we had run down the cobbled streets to Joshua's family silversmith shop in the Jewish quarter west of the Mezquita's towering walls of Cordoba. I knew that it would be only a matter of moments before they would find this hidden underground sanctuary. I took his delicate face with his large inquisitive brown eyes and said, "Joshua, I must take you to another place away from here."

"But my grandparents and my sister, what of them?"

"You must trust me, child. The Inquisition will claim your grandparents because they will not forsake their faith."

Clamping his slender little hands to cover his face he said, "No. Please, no. Does not the Church allow for confession, penances and conversions?"

"The Spanish monarchy now decrees all aspects of the Inquisition. The Holy Church is no longer involved. One word of a neighbor's accusations and those who are believed to be protected by the Inquisition's authority shall be burned at the stake."

"No, may not my family be spared? Can you not stop this from happening?"

I did not tell Joshua of my prayer for his family – that they be shown mercy by being garroted before burning – for if they were not, then they would be burned alive. I held him close and whispered, "I may not stop what the fates have already placed in motion."

"Is my whole family doomed?"

"Your sister shall be spared."

He managed a smile and said, "Truly?"

"Yes, truly. I know this as I know your sister will love a Christ figure with such a passion that she will become a nun and one day fulfill her destiny to sainthood."

"May I see her again? May I hold her and tell her that I love her?"

"It would not be wise or safe." I could tell from his visage that my answer distressed him, so I said, "I see the past, present, and future, and I must insist that you release the desire to see any family member that still might be alive. It is for your benefit."

"Can you also send messages from the beyond as a form of prayer?"

"Yes."

"Will you help me to do this?"

"What do you wish your supplication to convey, dearest child?"

A large tear rolled down his cheek as he sobbed and said, "On the wings of angels my prayer is to bless my dear sister and for her to hold my love in her heart." His beseeching eyes searched my face as he intently waited for my response. "Do you promise she will always know of my love for her?"

"I promise that she will know for all of eternity of your love."

"I beseech you to send the same prayer for my father and mother and all of those who will meet the fate you speak of. Will they too know of my eternal love? Do you promise?"

"Yes. I make you this vow and wish for you to feel peace for your loved ones."

I watched as he looked away and pondered the magnitude of what I had said. Slowly he turned to gaze at my face and said. "I have lost much, Mistress Ambriel. May I not, like you, see the past, present and future? Would not my heart hurt less if I had the gift of this sight you speak of? And would I not be more suited to fulfill my destiny if I had this gift?"

"The gift of seeing the future is not yours Joshua. You must believe me. Now I must remove you to a land far from here where you will continue to learn as your father and uncle desired."

"Is he dead – my uncle?"

"He will be soon, Joshua."

"Will his death like my parents' and my grandparents' be because of faith?"

"Yes. They are accused of being crypto-Jews, and, since the papal bill of 1483 expelling all Jews from Andalusia the persecutions have intensified. Your family knew it would only be a matter of time."

"Why? Why can Jews not practice their faith? For decades all faiths flourished. Even when the Moors ruled Spain Jews were free to express their beliefs. Twenty six years have since passed when the Pope made his decree – why do they continue to hunt us down?"

"The history of humankind is not always of forward motion. Many times fear darkens the progressive momentum of lessons already learned and a new form of a dark age thunders in to rule."

"I understand only some of what you say, Ambriel."

"I know, child. I also know that you are far wiser than your 13 years, but you cannot yet fully comprehend all that I have imparted to you."

"Make me know all. Make me know all now! I believe you can. Let it be so."

"Patience, Joshua. I have given you wisdom. You will know all that you need to know in good time." I held him close and said, "Are you ready to go to your new home?"

"Will the language of this land be known to me?"

"Dear Joshua, just as you mastered the tongue of English to speak as I speak so shall you have the skills of your new home."

A twinkle captured within his continence demonstrated immediately that this remarkable young lad had yet another boon to ask of me, for he said, "May I barter to gain some memory while you remove others?"

"Joshua, Joshua what manner of mischief courses through your high spirited mind?"

He smiled as he said, "Would it not be your blessing that I have the knowledge of many languages, Miss Ambriel? A blessing of the gift of many tongues would allow me to share my wisdoms with many more, would it not?"

I only needed a few seconds to ascertain his wisdom and answer him, as I said, "Yes, this request is appropriate and noble." As I placed my cupped palms over the top of his curly, golden brown locks, Joshua was imbued with all manner of language skills. When the task was complete, I said, "You have received the boon of languages, as you asked."

"May I speak all now?"

I laughed at his sweet excitement and said, "The ability to speak all other languages will come in a brief time. To your friends and family it will appear that you have a natural gift to learn, and you shall be encouraged to do so. Be patient with yourself and others, dear one."

After several moments of deep contemplation, he said, "Am I not bound to work hard to fulfill this, my destiny?" His furrowed brow showed his worried concern as he said, "Must I not labor and dedicate all my being to achieve what you speak of?"

I tousled his hair as I said, "Yes, but you are also bound to enjoy life and be a happy young boy. You will have many years in which to do as you are predestined."

"Truly?"

"Yes, truly." The voices of those who searched for Joshua were getting closer. "We must leave. Are you ready?"

"I am afraid."

"You have no reason to fear. I promise you will be in a place of love and have an opportunity to learn and grow and become the man you are destined to be," I said as I took him up into my arms.

He hugged my neck with trusting tenacity and whispered, "May God bless us all. I am ready."

I placed him in a trance, and a touch to his temples altered our oscillation so we became invisible. Men stomped into the cellar. I tarried only long enough to watch as confusion erupted when they found Joshua's cape and my heavy hooded cloak on the wooden bench. Details of how this precious cargo was transported are not necessary to our story. It was done. My charge was taken from the insanity of the Inquisition of Andalusia, Spain, only to awaken in a chair in a room in the serenity of Switzerland, next to a bed.

A young boy Joshua's age was in the bed, dead. When Joshua was fully awake, I caressed his beguiling face and said, "In a few moments, you shall be with your new mother and father."

"New mother and father? How can this be?"

"These wonderful people have only just come to the city. He is a learned chemist, physician and alchemist, not unlike your father and your uncle. It was destined for their young son to die and you to take his place."

"Shall they not know I am not their child?"

"No, dear one. Your memories and their memories shall become as memories of a cherished loving family. All shall be like a garden; in this garden you shall grow, learn and flourish."

He smiled a sad smile and said, "I shall trust you as my parents trusted you." He held tightly to my neck. "May I not see you again one day, my Mistress Ambriel?"

"I will sojourn to this dimension to visit."

"May I have a memory – will I know you?"

"When you do see me you will know that I am a part of your destiny, and this will give you peace," I said as I leaned closer and pulled him to my breast to comfort him.

He kissed me on the cheek and smiled. "I am now prepared to fulfill my destiny and be as I must be."

With a touch to his temples, I placed him in a trance. I changed Joshua out of his moss green breeches, bark brown doublet and cream colored sleeveless linen tunic and put him in the billowing white sleeping gown of the other boy. In respectful gentleness, I removed the dead child and placed Joshua on the cushioned pillows.

A woman's voice echoed from the hall, "Doctor, you must make him well."

Gathered in my arms the dead boy and I oscillated into a significantly higher vibration than visible to the human eye. As the boy's parents and his doctor entered the room, I swiftly altered memories of all present. I watched long enough to see joy and love shared between this now bonded family and to hear the doctor as he said, "You young parents should not over excite yourselves, Herr Von Hohenheim. Your wife wished for reassurance when consulting me. You are a fine physician, but you are the boy's father. Your son is sound of limb. See how his cheeks are like apples."

With a hearty bear hug, the father lifted the boy out of the bed and said, "Phillipus, my boy, you are alive."

"Papa . . . I . . . ." He hugged his father's neck and turned to his mother and said, "Mother, why do you weep?"

The three embraced in a unified family circle, and I returned to my world, knowing my task was accomplished.

THE SEVENTH JACKET
by Mary Ann Hutchison

The little tailor stitched the label directly underneath the small inside pocket of the seventh jacket and then placed his creation on the dressmaker's dummy. He reread the written instructions received eleven months prior, though by now he knew them by heart, and after being satisfied that he'd once more done as instructed, stepped back and admired his work.

As he concentrated on threading another needle, he thought back to a year ago. Three large cartons, each containing a bolt of expensive, light brown cashmere material, and a smaller carton containing seven flattened boxes meant to hold one man's dress jacket, had been mysteriously delivered to his shop in Santo Domingo. A pre-addressed typewritten mailing label was affixed to each box. There was no return address label.

Forensic examinations to determine the existence of fingerprints on the boxes would, later on, prove fruitless.

The instructions in the accompanying typewritten letter were specific: the tailor was to make seven jackets, using the exact measurements and style as directed. The jacket label could indicate that it had been made in the Dominican Republic (the only tribute to his handiwork the tailor was allowed) but could not contain his name or the name of his shop.

Included with the directions were seven squares of intricately folded notepaper. The tailor was to place one square into the small inside pocket of each jacket without reading it and then sew the pocket shut. The words "without reading it" were typed in bold letters and underlined for added emphasis. The meaning was not lost on the diminutive clothes maker.

When the work was completed, he was to carefully fold the jackets into the boxes provided and randomly mail them from various post offices in the neighboring country of Haiti. He was warned never to speak of this transaction or, if the directions were not followed exactly, dire consequences would result. A second envelope containing cash equal to three years' steady income was also included.

The letter was signed "John Smith," there was no return address on either the letter or its envelope. The tailor thought the entire transaction very strange, but the money overshadowed any doubts he might have had. He was not the richest of tailors, and he had a very large family to feed.

Why he'd been chosen to perform this task was never revealed to him. Since he would never be able to speak of what he considered to be a great honor, he'd decided that every stitch would be perfect and that no matter what commissions followed, these seven jackets would always be his finest work.

As he placed the last note into the pocket of the seventh jacket, curiosity overcame caution. He furtively looked around his shop, half expecting to see a shadowy stranger watching him from a dark corner; then he slowly unfolded the note. The typewritten message read: "When you find this, go to the address written below and tell the person answering the door that Mr. Smith sent you. Because you are an outstanding individual, you will receive a unique gift." It was signed, "An Anonymous Admirer." The little tailor carefully refolded the note, placed it inside the pocket and with precision and pride, sewed the pocket shut.

He smiled. How lucky I am to be part of such a wonderful surprise. Whoever Mr. Smith is, he must truly be a special person.

The next day, the tailor and his wife traveled just over the border into Haiti and shipped all seven boxes to the United States. Then they chose a very nice restaurant, one they normally couldn't afford, did a bit of shopping and returned to Santo Domingo. If his wife was curious, she did not show it. Although she was proud of her husband's tailoring ability, the business bored her. She accepted this unusual day as a gift without question.

Over the course of the next two years, six newspapers in six different locations in the United States would report the mysterious shooting deaths of six members of a particular gangland family. Other than the organized crime link, the only other tie to their deaths was the odd fact that each victim was wearing the same exact type of jacket — fabric, color, style and quality of tailoring were identical, down to the Dominican Republic label.

In Arizona, the seventh jacket was found hanging on the back of a chair after a conference of mortgage brokers had ended. The jacket, which was new to the wearer, had not as yet become a favorite in his wardrobe and had been easily forgotten.

His next door neighbor's daughter had given it to him about two weeks prior. The neighbor, a reclusive sort, had passed away in his sleep on the same day that a package containing the brown jacket had been delivered to him. The daughter, noting that her father and his neighbor were almost the same size, gave him the jacket since there was no way for her to return it — there was nothing to indicate where it came from or why it had been sent.

The stitches on the small inside pocket were not removed. There didn't seem any need to. It wasn't big enough to hold anything, really.

ABOUT THE AUTHORS

Carol Costa

  Carol Costa is an award-winning playwright and a journalist. Carol has worked as an editor of books and newspapers, a business news correspondent, and managed a literary agency.

  Carol's plays have been published and produced in New York City, Los Angeles, and regional theaters across the country. She has also worked as the Artistic Director of a community theater and currently runs a Readers Theater.

  Her published books include:

    Ask Aunt Emma, Champagne Books
    Invisible Force, Champagne Books
    The Master Plan, Avalon Books
    A Deadly Hand, Avalon Books
    Love Steals the Scene, Avalon Books
    Labor of Love, Avalon Books
    Teach Yourself Accounting in 24 Hours,
      1st & 2nd editions, Penguin USA
    The Complete Idiot's Guide to Surviving Bankruptcy,
      Penguin USA
    Teach Yourself Bookkeeping in 24 Hours, Penguin USA
    Video Poker: Play Longer with Less Risk, ECW Press
    The Complete Idiot's Guide to Starting and Running a
      Thrift Store, Penguin USA

  Her play, *The Last Decent Crooks*, is available through Big Dog Publishing.

Mary Ann Hutchison

  Hailing from the Midwest, Mary Ann Hutchison is a transplanted Wisconsinite who spent over 40 years in the legal field as: a legal secretary, Administrative Assistant for the Pima County Sheriff's Department, Courtroom Clerk and Judicial Administrative Assistant for the Pima County Superior Court.

After retiring she began to seriously put words on paper and writes short stories, memoirs, middle-grade, and suspense stories.

One husband, two spoiled felines, six children, 16 grandchildren, and five great-grandchildren constitute her immediate family. Her writing family derives from her affiliation with the Society of Southwestern Authors as a former member of its Board of Directors, serving as coordinator of the Society's media promotion and writing contest. She is a past Presiding Chair of Arizona Mystery Writers.

Her short stories and memoirs are included in "Good Old Days" magazines, *Thanksgiving to Christmas: A Patchwork of Stories*, and Arizona Mystery Writers anthology, *A Way With Murder*. Her latest novel, *Moochi's Mariachis* is now available from Open Books Press.

Jude Johnson

Jude Johnson is a "Native by Proxy" Arizonan who loves history, fantasy, and learning crazy languages such as Welsh. She is the author of *Dragon & Hawk*, book one of a historical adventure/romance series set in 1880s Southern Arizona and due for publication by Champagne Books in April 2011 (**www.champagnebooks.com**), with two sequels ready to follow. She also writes romance/erotica as Nia Little.

Find her at her **website: www.scorchedhawkpress.com**; on Facebook at **www.facebook.com/jude.johnson**; and on My Space at **www.myspace.com/judeaz.**

Ashleen O'Gaea ("pronounce it *oh-jee-uh*")

Ashleen O'Gaea is a 60% native Tucsonan and a long-time writer. She has written several books about Wicca, including *The Family Wicca Book, Raising Witches*, and a two-volume set, *Celebrating the Seasons of Life*. In 2010 she broke into fiction with *The Green Boy* and *The Flower Bride*. The third book in the Bliss Harper-Coyote Song series, *Maiden, Vampire, Crone* came out at the end of 2010. Her books are available through various sources, including CreateSpace, Amazon, Smashwords, Barnes&Noble, and Circle Sanctuary.

O'Gaea also writes a column for *Witches&Pagans* magazine, and as a fully-ordained Wiccan priestess leads workshops and performs Sabbats and passage rites. She is on-line at **www.AshleenOGaea.com**, **www.PentagramConsulting.net** and on Facebook.

D.H. Tremont

D.H. Tremont is well suited for writing international intrigue. She obtained a degree in Theatre Production and studied at the University of Loyola in Rome, Italy. She also lived in England and studied in Cambridge. Ms. Tremont has traveled to over 50 countries, returning to favorite locations whenever possible. Living in Rome, Italy for many years and coming from Italian ancestry makes Tremont's complete understanding of this amazing city palpable when reading her books. She has friends and connections with people in Mossad, Interpol, the Polizia which is also known as the Questura in Italy, to name but a few of the sources she has used and continues to utilize to make her books credible and accurate. Her contacts in the Carabinieri have helped with her research pertaining to art theft and related subjects.